LORENZO'S
SECRET MISSION

Lila Guzmán
and
Rick Guzmán

PIÑATA

BOOKS

PIÑATA BOOKS
ARTE PÚBLICO PRESS
HOUSTON, TEXAS

This volume is made possible through grants from the National Endowment for the Arts (a federal agency), the Andrew W. Mellon Foundation, and the City of Houston through The Cultural Arts Council of Houston, Harris County.

Piñata Books are full of surprises!

Piñata Books

An imprint of
Arte Público Press
University of Houston
452 Cullen Performance Hall
Houston, Texas 77204-2004

Cover illustration by Roberta Collier-Morales.
Cover design by Giovanni Mora.

Guzmán, Lila, 1952–
    Lorenzo's Secret Mission / by Lila and Rick Guzmán.
        p.   cm.
    Two historical figures, Bernardo De Gálvez and George Gibson, appear prominently in the book.
    Summary: In 1776, fifteen-year-old Lorenzo Bannister leaves Texas and his father's new grave to carry a letter to the Virginia grandfather he has never known, and becomes involved with the struggle of the American Continental Army and its Spanish supporters.
    ISBN 1-55885-341-3
        1. Gálvez, Bernardo De, 1746–1786—Juvenile fiction.   2. Gibson, George, 1747–1791—Juvenile fiction.   3. United States—History—Revolution, 1775–1783—Fiction.   4. Orphans—Fiction.
    5. Identity—Fiction.   6. Slavery—Fiction.]   I. Guzmán, Rick and Lila.   II. Title.
    PZ7.G9885 Lo 2001
    [Fic]—dc21   2001034006
                                                                                                        CIP

⊚ The paper used in this publication meets the requirements of the American National Standard for Information Sciences—Permanence of Paper for Printed Library Materials, ANSI Z39.48-1984.

1 2 3 4 5 6 7 8 9 0   10 9 8 7 6 5 4 3 2 1

In Memory of
Angelita Guzmán
(October 2, 1916–September 19, 1999)
and
Gibson's Lambs,
forgotten heroes of the American Revolution

Acknowledgments

Our thanks go to Susan Rockhold, Helen Ginger, Laura Chávez, and Ross Sams for reading and critiquing *Lorenzo's Secret Mission;* to Milord Writer, Vince McCarthy, an Englishman and horror writer who cheerfully accepted the task of making sure the British sounded British; to Dr. James Sidbury of the University of Texas for sharing his knowledge of slavery in Virginia.

⟫ ⟫ ⟫

Lorenzo's Secret Mission is based on a true story. George Washington, Bernardo De Gálvez, George Gibson, and William Linn are historical figures. All other characters are fictional.

Chapter One

From my hiding place in the moon-cast shadows, I surveyed a forest of ships anchored in New Orleans' harbor. Some, I knew, would sail to faraway ports, to Spain, or Cuba, or maybe the Two Floridas. I had to find a ship bound for Virginia and get on board somehow, even if that meant becoming a stowaway.

A long knife, bullet pouch, powder-horn, and canteen hung at my side. My most treasured possessions lay at my feet. Papá's medical bag, a flintlock musket he gave me for my birthday two years ago, and a small raccoon-skin haversack containing Papá's papers.

On his deathbed, Papá wrote a letter to my grandfather in Virginia. "This letter is important, Lorenzo," my father had said when he handed it to me. "Promise me you will deliver it."

"Upon my word of honor, I shall," I had replied.

Visibly relieved, Papá said, "Your future and the future of many others will depend on that letter. I shall soon join your mother in heaven. You must make your own way in the world. Be brave, Lorenzo. Be a man of honor."

"I'll make you proud of me, Papá."

And then he was gone. Two weeks ago, the afternoon of August 7, 1776, I buried my father at a Spanish mission in San Antonio and set out for Virginia.

On the way to New Orleans I had trudged through swamps so spongy, I sank up to my boot tops in mud

1

and slime. Clouds of mosquitoes attacked me. Worst of all, I had to keep a sharp eye out for snakes and gators.

Now, rested and ready to set out again, I pushed a lock of hair back in place and adjusted the frayed ribbon that held my hair in a pigtail at my neck. I gripped my musket, picked up my possessions, and headed toward the wharf.

Across the street, a party was under way. Harpsichord music drifted through the open windows of a two-story house about thirty yards away. A gray, thin-faced man bowed low to a smiling girl dressed all in white. She dropped him a dainty curtsey, and they began to dance a minuet.

I'd never seen a girl with hair the color of a desert sunset. I crossed the street to get a better view and stood beneath a cypress tree. She was fifteen or so, about my age, but her partner looked old enough to be her grandfather. She stared in my direction. I jumped, but realized she couldn't see me in the dark.

Compared to the dancers in silk and satin, I was a sorry sight indeed. The trek had left my buckskin britches and flannel shirt tattered and sweat-stained, my face soiled, and my hair tangled. I stank worse than a wet dog.

The steamy night plastered my shirt to my back. With my sleeve, I mopped away sweat. I uncorked my canteen and took a long drink of water.

Easing past the Customs House, one of the few buildings clearly marked, I slipped down to the wharf so I could look over the ships. Their flags would tell me their place of origin and give me a clue as to their destination.

Papá had warned me about press gangs that captured young men and forced them to serve aboard His Britannic Majesty's ships, so I stayed out of sight. At fifteen years old, I was just what they'd be looking for.

The wharf was busier than I expected. It reminded me of a beehive. Hugging the shadows, I watched, fascinated.

At the far end of the crescent-shaped harbor, the red-and-gold flag of Spain flew from a warship's highest mast. I knew that flag well. Back home in San Antonio, it waved over the army barracks.

Large, square lanterns placed at regular intervals along the wharf lit a path to a warehouse. Bare-chested sailors rolled barrels down a wooden gangplank to men in buckskin, moccasins, and coonskin caps.

How peculiar. Who would unload a ship in the middle of the night? I placed Papá's medical bag and my haversack on the ground, leaned my shoulder against the side of a building, and watched with growing interest.

Barrel after barrel rumbled down the ramp. Huge men rolled them on the wharf to two Spanish officers waiting by the warehouse. One watched the barrels disappear through open double doors while the other jotted something down in a log.

On our travels around New Spain and the Province of Texas, Papá had told me stories about pirates who buried chests full of Spanish doubloons on tropical islands and smuggled molasses and French wine into the British colonies.

These men were probably pirates. Bits of their conversation drifted toward me. The sailors spoke Spanish while their companions used English.

When I heard "General Washington," I perked right up. Papá had talked about him often. Washington was a fellow Virginian, Papá said, the leader of the British colonists who had begun a revolt against King George.

A large barrel thumped down the wooden ramp and drew my attention back to the ship.

"*Hijo de la—*" began the sailor who had lost his hold on the barrel. Before he could finish his terrible oath, it wobbled to the end of the ramp and crashed into another barrel, narrowly missing one of the men. The impact sounded like a clap of thunder.

The lids burst off both barrels. Out spilled a grainy substance that looked like gunpowder. It made my nose twitch. I laid my finger under it to stifle a sneeze.

A giant of a man in buckskin rushed forward. "Careful!" he said in a menacing growl. He grabbed the two sailors by the scruff of the neck and shook them. "One mistake could blow us to Kingdom Come."

The two sailors righted the barrels while the buckskin-clad men closest to the accident fell to their knees and scooped up powder.

As they worked, the big man glanced over his shoulder to see who might have witnessed the accident.

At that second, I heard a sound at my back. Instinctively, I reached for my knife.

Cold metal pressed against the back of my head.

"Drop your weapons," a voice growled in my ear.

I drew a deep breath and eased my musket onto the wooden planks. Next, I unsheathed my knife and laid it beside my musket.

"Put your hands up!" My captor seized me by the collar. "Move, dog!" His grip tightened. He propelled me forward, down the wharf, toward the warehouse, and the Spanish officers waiting there.

Chapter Two

The pirates continued to unload the ship. Lucky for me, they hadn't noticed us yet. Close by, their muskets lay stacked in a teepee-like shape.

How long would it take the men to reach their muskets, snatch them up, load, and fire if I managed to bolt away? Thirty seconds if they knew their business. Sixty, if they didn't.

A spiteful, hard shove from behind made me stumble. Seeing my opportunity to escape, I bent low and jabbed my elbow backwards as hard as I could into my captor's stomach. He yipped like a coyote.

Weaving and bobbing, I raced toward the darkened streets opposite the wharf, funneling all my energy into running. I glanced over my shoulder as I crossed the square and took a sharp intake of breath.

The pirate had recovered from the blow and was after me. In a burst of speed, I dashed down the alley between the cathedral and a three-story building, rounded the corner, and headed up a long, cobblestone street. I felt like a deer running through a narrow valley to escape from hunters. Boots thudded behind me.

The next time I glanced back, I noticed I had put distance between us. Unfortunately, two men had joined the pursuit, although they were still much farther back.

Deeper and deeper into the city I ran until my chest ached. I had to find a place to rest and take cover. At the next corner loomed a two-story house, its windows dark. Moonlight fell on the lush garden around it. This was as good a place as any to stop while I caught my breath and figured out what to do next.

I pulled up short and dived behind a bank of oleanders. To my surprise, brick pillars raised the house three feet or so off the ground. Perfect! I ducked down and scooted between the pillars. In a matter of seconds, I crawled to the central one. My breath whooshed in and out. I forced myself to lie still, face down, and control my panting. It had been close, very close, and I wasn't safe yet. A quick vision of walking the plank of a pirate ship leaped to mind.

Seconds later, my ears picked up an unusual sound. Alarmed, I strained to hear better and inched forward to peep out. Moonlight streamed through the leaves and twining vines that concealed me. I spied a giant in buckskin and moccasins walking toe to heel like an Indian, his face veiled in darkness.

My heart hammered. I crouched down, ready to bolt if necessary.

He stood still, studied the ground, looked all around, then started to edge past me. Just then, a man in boots pounded toward him. I watched in horror as they both stopped about three feet away.

"What do you think?" a deep voice asked in hushed tones.

"I think we've lost him."

"Did you get a good look at him?"

"Yes. I'll know him the next time I see him."

"One thing's for sure. He can run like the devil."

The boots shifted. Another pair of moccasins joined them.

The deep voice suddenly slipped into English. "See anything, William?"

"No. Looks like he got away. We'd better return to the ship and see how the men are doing."

"I agree." He turned to the man in boots and talked to him in Spanish.

I couldn't see their faces, but I memorized their voices. Apparently, the man in boots spoke only Spanish and one of the men in moccasins spoke only English. The deep-voiced man knew both Spanish and English and interpreted for them.

Both sets of moccasins shuffled off together while the boots headed in the opposite direction. They had given up! I heaved a sigh of relief.

And then something awful struck me. The haversack with the letter to my grandfather. And my father's medical bag. I had lost them on the wharf. Where were they now? How could I recover them? It was too dangerous to go back and look for them now.

I stretched out full length upon the ground, pillowed my head on my crossed arms, and closed my eyes, disappointed in myself. Less than an hour after entering New Orleans, I had lost everything.

The ground, moist and soft, gave off an offensive odor, the smell of decay, but I didn't care. Too tired to keep my eyes open any longer, I fell asleep wondering how I would get my possessions back.

Chapter Three

Loud voices coming from the house directly over-head awoke me the next morning. Dappled sunlight filtered through the greenery and touched my face.

"I'm awake, Papá," I mumbled. Looking around, I suddenly remembered I wasn't in San Antonio with Papá.

Sore from sleeping on the ground, I stretched life back into my limbs. First order of the day, find my possessions. Second, get on a ship to Virginia.

Mulling this over, I trudged downhill toward the dark brown Mississippi and wove in and out of the crowded streets leading to the harbor. Along the way, I passed a schoolhouse where I could hear children chanting their lessons. Then I passed a convent, a cathedral, and a jail.

A warm breeze carried the fragrance of jasmine and magnolia. I drew a deep breath. Somewhere not too far off, someone was brewing coffee. I breathed deeper. What tantalizing aromas.

I passed a reluctant school boy, sailors, and customs officials. Close by, Indians squatted on colorful blankets and sold baskets of sassafras root. A black man, shirtless and gleaming with sweat, pushed a two-wheeled cart loaded with empty glass bottles to the river's edge.

People stepped out of the way when they saw me approach and gave me long, curious looks.

Compared to San Antonio, New Orleans was a big city. San Antonio consisted of little more than a frontier fort, a Spanish mission, and twenty or so families. New Orleans throbbed with people, all speaking a confusion of languages. It struck me that New Orleans appeared somewhat more civilized than San Antonio, although both were only about fifty years old.

On the eight-foot levee that sloped to the river, I paused. The pirate ship I'd stumbled upon last night had unloaded its cargo and left. A lucky break, especially if the giant and his crew had left, too.

I walked to the last place I had my possessions and looked all about, but my luck didn't hold. Someone had already taken them. Even without Papá's letter, I still had to go to Virginia. My grandfather was my only living relative. So I slipped down to the Customs House, all the time watching for a red-coated British press gang. There, I scanned the huge chalkboard where the harbor master listed outbound ships. Spain. Cuba. France. My heart sank. Not a single ship bound for Virginia. I scowled up at the harbor master's board.

A girl with copper-colored hair stepped to my side. She spoke to me in French.

"I'm sorry," I replied in English with an apologetic smile. "I don't understand."

A look of disappointment crossed her face. "I said, what a face you make." She spoke in broken Spanish, her wide green eyes dancing with merriment. "Nothing could be quite so bad."

I stared at her in amazement and recognized her at once. She was the girl I'd seen dancing last night. She was even prettier up close. I'd never seen eyes so green or skin so creamy. She wore a straw hat and a white muslin dress.

"My name is Eugenie Dubreton," she said in a Spanish heavy with a French accent.

I swallowed hard and shifted from foot to foot. Not too long ago, I thought of girls as silly creatures that played with dolls and gave pretend tea parties, but recently my feelings toward them had started to shift. To make matters worse, here stood a beautiful girl, and I was less than presentable.

"I'm Lorenzo," I finally managed to squeak out in Spanish. "Lorenzo Bannister."

"*Enchantée*, Lorenzo," she said with a small smile. She eyed me a moment, then lowered her voice. "Are you one of Gibson's Lambs?"

"Who are Gibson's Lambs?"

"Fur traders from Pennsylvania." She turned toward the harbor master's board. "Are you going somewhere?"

"Virginia."

"That is a long way off."

"My grandfather lives there. I promised my father I'd deliver a letter to him." A dull ache came to my chest whenever I thought about Papá.

"And so you go to Virginia?"

"If I can find a ship."

"There is one leaving for Pennsylvania on October 2."

I looked back at the board. "It isn't listed."

She gave me a sly look. "Not yet. It will be. Pennsylvania is not far from Virginia, *n'est-ce pas*?"

If Eugenie was right about the ship, I had a month to kill. With not a Spanish pillar dollar to my name, I needed work and a place to stay.

Rain-swollen clouds darkened the southern horizon. Bits of trash skittered by, driven by a hot wind that stung my eyes. The rising gulf breeze threatened to blow away Eugenie's straw hat. She held it firmly on her head and clutched a cloth-covered basket a little tighter. "A storm is coming. I must hurry."

"Where are you headed?"

"Over there." She pointed to a bakery that faced the wharf.

I watched her walk off and scolded myself for not offering to escort her.

She took three steps, half turned, and waved for me

to catch up. My heart pounded like a wild mustang's hooves over the plain. I didn't need a second invitation.

About twenty feet away, a tavern sign creaked and groaned in the wind.

"My mistress has invited Colonel De Gálvez to dinner," she said, breaking the silence between us. "He simply adores French pastries."

"De Gálvez? Papá once doctored a man named Captain De Gálvez. He had two Apache spears in his chest and an arrow in his left arm. I wonder if he's related to Colonel De Gálvez."

Before Eugenie could respond, a loud, drunken song drew our attention to the tavern on our left. Three soldiers, reeling drunk, burst through the door. Two wore the blue of British marines. Their companion was a redcoat. The first one was short and plump; the second hunched over as if he were carrying a heavy burden; and the third, the tallest of the lot, bore a saber scar on his cheek that made him look dangerous. They sang, "Yankee Doodle went to London, riding on a pony, stuck a feather in his cap and called it macaroni!"

"Gawd!" the hunchback exclaimed. "Wish I was going to fight the Yankees."

"Wish I was going to Virginia with you," the short, fat one said. "Least they speak English there."

British marines! A chill went through me. Logic told me to run before they seized me and pressed me into service in the British navy. My sense of honor said to stay put and protect Eugenie. I hoped they were too drunk to notice us.

A gust of wind blew the taller soldier's hat into a mud puddle at my feet.

Saber-Scar looked at me and bellowed, "Hey, you! Diego! Fetch my hat!"

"Are you addressing me?" The words popped out in a flash of anger. How many times had Papá warned me to control my temper? More than I could remember.

"Look lively now," the hunchback said, "and he'll give you half-a-pence."

I glared defiance at him.

"I say," the third soldier said. "The bugger's not going to do it."

Saber-Scar staggered toward me. "Fetch my hat, boy!"

Now, only a distance of a few feet separated us.

"Fetch it yourself."

Surprise and anger turned his cheeks red. "Little monkey's barking mad. Thinks he's our equal."

"And got himself a regular lady!" the hunchbacked soldier exclaimed. "Come here, milady." He pulled Eugenie tight to him and laughed when she struggled to break free.

"Let her go!" I lunged at the man, but my attack was thwarted by the tall soldier, who seized me and pinned my arms behind me.

When Eugenie's captor tried to kiss her, she drew her head back and spat in his face. Livid, the man wiped away spittle, then slapped Eugenie hard. Her cry of pain made me fly into a blind rage. I stomped on Saber-Scar's foot. He cursed and twisted my arms upward until I thought they would snap.

At that instant, footsteps pounded toward us. I jerked my head toward the sound, surprised and glad to see a giant in buckskin, moccasins, and coonskin cap race forward. He stood at least six-feet-six. Dark-haired, fair-skinned, he was somewhere between twenty and thirty. At his side trotted a second man.

"I despise an uneven fight," the giant said, his face tight with anger.

"'Specially when it's with the Brits," his companion added. Tall, at least six feet, the second man appeared no more than seventeen or eighteen years old. He wore a puffy-sleeved white shirt and homespun trousers held up by suspenders.

"Bloody hell!" the hunchback exclaimed. "Yankee Doodles!"

At that, the giant struck the hunchback in the nose while his friend clobbered the third soldier.

Using the element of surprise, I bent forward and flipped my captor over my back. Together we fell head-long into the puddle. Covered with mud, I scrambled up a second before Saber-Scar did and lunged at him again.

It became a free-for-all. We jabbed, punched, kicked. I took one on the side of my head. Blood trickled into my eyes. I managed to hit Saber-Scar in the stomach with my right fist. His body jerked at the impact and doubled over. Before he could unfold himself, I gave him a two-fisted blow to the back of the neck. He sailed into the street, slid on the mud, and landed next to his hat.

Victory felt good until my hands began to hurt. I tried to shake it out. Just then, a squad of blue-jacketed Spanish soldiers rushed toward us.

"You are all under arrest for disturbing the peace!" the officer-in-charge announced as his soldiers leveled their muskets. "Put your hands up!"

We all raised our hands at the same time.

The Spanish officer retrieved Eugenie's basket and handed it to her. "Are you all right, dear?"

"I'm fine, thank you."

His expression changed from tender concern to anger as his eyes moved toward us. "Take them to jail!"

Saber-Scar uttered a terrible oath and shot me a murderous look. Under his breath, he said, "This is all your fault, Diego. I'll get you for this if it's the last thing I do."

Chapter Four

The Spanish officer-in-charge grabbed my collar and tightened his grip. "So we meet again."

My heart sank. I recognized his voice. Last night on the wharf, he had put a pistol to my head.

"Lieutenant Calderón!" Eugenie said, tugging on his jacket sleeve. "The British started it."

Ignoring her, he propelled me forward, across the green, toward jail, leaving the rest of his squad to deal with the others.

No doubt Lieutenant Calderón had singled me out because he remembered the elbow jab in the stomach. He shoved me through a wrought-iron gate, down a dark, twisting staircase, and into a dungeon cell that stank like an unemptied chamber pot.

Jail! I was in jail! I had never been in trouble with the law before. And my crime? Defending Eugenie from a band of bullies. Angry at the world for the unfairness of my arrest, I sank to the moldy straw on the dirt floor and buried my hands in my hair. I could imagine Papá looking down from heaven and shaking his head in disappointment. How was I going to get to Virginia now?

"Howdy, son!" The voice boomed from an enormous bulk in the corner. "Whatcha name?"

"Lorenzo."

"They call me Red. 'Cause of this."

In the thin light filtering through a narrow window, I could barely see the man gesture to his hair.

Fear darted up my spine when the man unfolded

himself. At five-foot-six, I was big for my age. Even so, my cellmate towered over me. His beard, dirty and uncombed, reached to his waist. He smelled like bear grease. Like the giant who had come to my rescue, he wore buckskin and moccasins.

The heavy wooden door opened and two men, pushed from behind, stumbled inside. My new cellmates turned out to be the men who had helped me fight Saber-Scar and his gang. The door clanged shut again.

"Cap'n Gibson!" Red exclaimed. "Whatcha doing here?"

The tallest man grinned at him. "Bit of a misunderstanding with the local authorities." He turned toward me and thrust out his hand. "I'm Captain Gibson."

I shook his hand and introduced myself. Was this *the* Gibson Eugenie had referred to and was Red one of his "Lambs"? If so, a lamb was the last thing Red resembled.

"What are you a captain of?" I asked, hoping Gibson commanded a ship bound for Virginia.

"A militia company. This gentleman," he said, "is my second-in-command, Lieutenant William Linn."

Gibson's lieutenant offered his hand. "A pleasure to meet you." His sandy-colored hair and pale gray-green eyes reminded me of Papá's.

Gibson slid down beside me and leaned his head against the rough stone wall while William Linn lowered himself to the ground and sat cross-legged across from us.

"You lead a charmed life, son," Gibson said.

"I'm in jail, Captain," I pointed out.

"Not for long. As soon as Colonel De Gálvez hears what you did, he'll let you go."

I offered him a doubtful look.

"I bet you a Spanish pillar dollar he'll turn you loose before nightfall."

"I'll take that bet," I said, even though I didn't have a Spanish pillar dollar to my name.

"That girl you rescued," Gibson said with a victorious grin, "is Eugenie Dubreton, the Widow De Saint Maxent's personal maid. And since Colonel De Gálvez is courting the widow . . ." He swirled his hand as if to say, "You figure it out."

"Oh."

Gibson laughed. "'Oh,' indeed. I'll bet you could fall in an outhouse and come up smelling like roses."

"I doubt that."

"If it's any consolation," Gibson said, raising his voice so the people in the next cell could hear, "the Lobsterbacks are in jail, too."

"Lobsterbacks!" an English voice cried out. He hurled vicious insults at us.

Gibson banged his fist on the wall. "Curb your tongue. There are gentlemen in this cell."

I assumed Gibson called them Lobsterbacks because most British soldiers wore scarlet coats. "Why do they call you Yankee Doodles?"

Gibson's mouth pulled into a tight line. "It's a scornful song the British sing to make fun of us. It's about an ignorant American who goes to town and makes a fool of himself. We are nothing to the British. A source of tax revenue. Stupid peasants they treat like stepchildren. When the British regulars fired on our minutemen at Lexington-Concord, they fired on British citizens."

I had never thought of it quite that way.

Saber-Scar's words echoed in my ears. "Thinks he's our equal." I had spoken to them in English. By my accent, they knew I was a British subject, a fellow citizen. And it hadn't mattered at all.

"Show Lorenzo your back," Gibson said to Red.

Without question, Red pulled the shirt over his head. He twisted toward the light.

Nausea gripped me when I saw his back, seamed and ridged with scars from his neck to his waistline. Scarcely any of his original skin remained.

"Red deserted from the British navy after they flogged him." Gibson's expression held a deep sadness. "The British will hang him if they ever catch him."

"I'm an American," Red said. "Ain't gonna be no man's slave."

My mouth went dry. I didn't blame him for deserting. Nor did I care what Red might or might not have done. No one deserved to be beaten so viciously.

Gibson smiled thinly. "You fought like a gator out there. Next time I'm in a fight, I want you on my side."

The key scraped in the lock and the door swung open. In one bound, the four of us—Red, Gibson, Linn, and I— leaped to our feet.

Lieutenant Calderón, the man that arrested us, stepped inside. He was tall and slender, not nearly as muscular as I, about nineteen or twenty years old. Square-jawed, with large brown eyes, he was pale, like most Spanish bluebloods. A long, straight nose dominated his face.

Behind him stood a round-faced man who looked important in a blue jacket heavy with gold braiding. He wore a white waistcoat and white knee breeches tucked into black knee boots. His sharp, black eyes slid from Red, to Gibson, to Linn, but remained the longest on me. His scowl deepened. "You. Step forward."

Chapter Five

Feeling like a criminal, I did as ordered. I ran a nervous hand through my mud-caked hair. "Yes, sir?"

Lieutenant Calderón took a menacing step toward me. "This gentleman is Colonel De Gálvez, captain general of Louisiana, you dolt! You will bow and address him as 'Your Excellency.'"

I blinked up at the colonel. Was this the man my father doctored five years ago? I saw no flicker of recognition in his eyes. I bowed low. "Your Excellency."

"Were you in a brawl with guards from the British embassy?" the colonel demanded.

I grimaced. "Yes, Your Excellency."

"Forevermore!" Colonel De Gálvez's eyes bored a hole in me. "You thought you could take on three soldiers all by yourself?"

Gibson spoke up. "He was defending Eugenie's honor."

"Yes. I know. She told me."

"Yes, sir." Gibson continued on. "Fighting all three of them himself when we chanced upon him."

That wasn't exactly how it happened. Saber-Scar had my arms pinned when Gibson and Linn came along, but I thought it best not to contradict Gibson.

"I can't thank you enough, gentlemen," Colonel De Gálvez said in a suddenly choked voice. "You are free to go."

Gibson whispered over my shoulder, "You owe me a Spanish pillar dollar."

His remark brought a smile to my face. My smile widened to see Lieutenant Calderón slap his gloves against his thighs in exasperation over our release. He wheeled around and stalked away.

Gibson and Linn made a motion to go, but Red didn't move a muscle.

"You, too, Red," Colonel De Gálvez said.

Red hurried out with William Linn.

Colonel De Gálvez signaled for me and Gibson to remain. His gaze met mine. "Eugenie told me your name is Lorenzo Bannister. Is that correct?"

"Yes, Your Excellency."

"What is your father's name?"

"Jack Bannister, Your Excellency."

The colonel hunched down to eye level with me. "*Dr.* Bannister?"

"Yes, Your Excellency."

"Lorenzo," Colonel De Gálvez said in a surprised voice. "I didn't recognize you. You've grown. Eugenie said you were trying to get on a ship going to Virginia." His expression grew stern. "Does your father know you're running away to sea?"

"No, sir, he doesn't. I mean . . ." My gaze fell. "My father is dead."

Colonel De Gálvez drew a ragged breath. "I held Jack in high esteem. I am grieved to learn of his passing."

My throat tightened. I was proud to hear a man of Colonel De Gálvez's stature praise my father.

"How does a gentleman's son come to be in . . . such a state?" He seemed at a loss for words to describe my condition.

"My father was taking me to my grandfather in Virginia, but we had to stop in San Antonio when he became too ill to travel on. He's buried there." At that point, my voice cracked. I swallowed hard and pressed my lips together.

For months, Papá couldn't work. With no money coming in and expenses for his medical care mounting, we soon spent our savings. Whenever I could, I worked on a friend's cattle ranch to earn extra money.

Colonel De Gálvez laid a gentle hand on my shoulder. "I'm sorry, Lorenzo. When did Jack pass away?"

"Two weeks ago. I set out for Virginia after his funeral."

"Through Indian territory?" Gibson asked in an awe-filled tone. "Was anyone with you?"

"No, sir."

Gibson's face reflected a sudden, deep interest. "You were all alone? What did you eat?"

"Squirrel, rabbit, dove. I shot whatever I could find and broiled it over the fire. Each night I slept beneath the stars, and each morning I started out before dawn. I made good time until my mare stepped in a hole and broke her leg about a hundred miles outside San Antonio. The rest of the trip was on foot."

"Forevermore." Admiration tinged Colonel De Gálvez's voice. "First Cabeza de Vaca walked across Texas, and now you."

Captain Gibson looked equally impressed. "In the summer, no less."

The colonel gently squeezed my shoulder. "If it weren't for your father, I wouldn't be alive today. I owe him a debt of gratitude I have never sufficiently repaid. Seeing you to Virginia gives me the chance to do that. However, I cannot in good conscience send you by ship. During wartime, travel on the high seas is dangerous. British warships are all along the Atlantic coast. I know of a better way to get you to Virginia." In the long pause that followed, his gaze drifted to Gibson, who bobbed his head in slow, silent agreement.

"Let's retire to my office and discuss this," the colonel suggested.

We headed upstairs to the jail's top floor.

A few minutes later, Colonel De Gálvez settled into a plush armchair behind a giant mahogany desk and waved me into a slatted chair across from it. "He's all yours, Captain."

Gibson, standing to his right with hands knotted behind him, studied me through narrowed eyes. "Have you ever been on a flatboat?"

"No, sir. What's a flatboat?"

"Well," Gibson began, "it's a boat with a flat bottom that moves goods up and down the Mississippi."

I now recalled seeing a rectangular-shaped cargo boat arrive at the dock just before I met Eugenie. So that was a flatboat.

"Was your father training you to become a physician?"

"Yes, sir. I was his apprentice."

"What is licorice good for?"

"Diarrhea, among other things."

Gibson grunted. "And St. John's Wort?"

"It's for aches and pains in arms, legs, and hips. Depression, too."

"*Tu ne cede malis sed . . .*" Gibson cocked an eyebrow and whirled his hand at me as if to say "finish it."

" . . . *contra audentior ito.*" The Latin quotation came from Virgil's *Aeneid* and stated, "Yield not to misfortunes, but advance all the more boldly against them." I eyed Captain Gibson suspiciously. He was testing me. Speaking the classic languages marked a well-educated man.

"Can you swim?"

The question jolted me. "What?" Realizing how rude that sounded, I quickly added the word "sir."

"Can you swim?" he repeated.

"Yes, sir."

Colonel De Gálvez and Gibson again exchanged glances.

Head bent, deep in thought, Gibson paced back and forth in front of me. "A medic who can swim." He stopped long enough to help himself to a cigar from an elegant wooden box on the colonel's desk.

"Have a cigar, Captain," the colonel said dryly.

Gibson grinned and lit it off an oil lamp. He pivoted toward me and his grin vanished. "What do you know about the war against King George?"

I didn't immediately answer. Captain Gibson's questions appeared illogical at best.

"In San Antonio, we heard the colonists won the Battle of Lexington and Concord but lost a little later at Bunker Hill. We heard about the Boston Tea Party, too."

How Papá and I had laughed when we learned angry colonists, dressed like Mohican Indians, had smeared their faces with gunpowder and dumped a shipload of British tea in the harbor to protest high taxes. Beaver and Eleanor were the names of the ships.

"The colonies signed a declaration of independence on the fourth of July," Gibson said. "The war has turned into a full-fledged revolution. If you were to take sides, would you favor the British or the colonists?"

By now, a stormy darkness had settled on New Orleans. Raindrops lashed the window panes. The oil lamp sent shadows leaping around the room.

I focused on them while I pondered my answer. "My mother was Mexican, but my father was a Virginian. In fact, he knew some of the rebels."

Gibson frowned at the glowing tip of his cigar. "You sidestepped the question. Which side do you favor? British or American?"

I remembered Papá shaking his head after reading Mr. Jefferson's most recent letter. "Tom is going to get himself hanged for treason," Papá had muttered. He was silent for a long time after that, his eyes unfocused as if lost in thought.

Gibson's dark blue eyes glinted in the lamplight. "You are not alone in your confusion. Many of the colonists have not yet declared their loyalties. In some cases, it has caused ruptures within families. My father-in-law is a British sympathizer. When I joined the Continental Army, he called me a traitor to King George." Gibson smiled bitterly. "As well as other names not repeatable. The wounds between us may never heal."

"I saw the scars on Red's back," I said, "and the way Saber-Scar and his friends treated me. I think the United Colonies should rebel."

Gibson gave me a satisfied smile. "We are now the United States of America." He took my hand in a long, firm grasp. "Welcome aboard, son."

Colonel De Gálvez leaned forward, his hands steepled before him. "I want your word of honor as a gentleman that none of what you now hear will leave this room."

"You have it, Your Excellency."

After a thoughtful moment, he said, "The dogs of war have been unleashed. Spain, like France, has not yet taken sides. It is inevitable that both will oppose the British for their own reasons. The French are still stinging from their defeat in the French and Indian War. Do you know why New Orleans is now a Spanish city?"

"No, Your Excellency."

"The French built it, but fourteen years ago, at the end of the French and Indian War, they secretly gave it to us to keep it out of English hands. The King of Spain is encouraging the Americans to rebel. However, until he declares war on Britain, any help he gives them must be kept secret. Captain Gibson and his men are here on a mission to take supplies to Washington and his rebels."

I straightened. "What kind of supplies?"

"Quinine to combat smallpox. Sulphur, saltpeter, flints, lead, gunpowder, muskets, cloth, and other stores."

"Cloth?"

Colonel De Gálvez smiled at my look of incredulity. "Few of Washington's soldiers have proper uniforms.

The trading firm of Gardoqui and Sons in Spain for-
warded military stores to Havana, Cuba. They arrived
last night and were warehoused. Gibson's Lambs will
take them up the Mississippi by flatboat."

I stared at him in admiration and amazement. The
Spanish were secretly funneling war supplies upriver to
General Washington. So that was what I had chanced
upon last night. They weren't pirates at all.

"The flatboats are the last leg of the journey," he went
on. "And the most dangerous. The flotilla needs a medic.
You need to get to your grandfather in Virginia. This will
be mutually beneficial. Are you interested?"

I leaped from my chair. "Am I, sir! Sure am! Sign me
on. When do we leave?"

Chapter Six

A month later, on September 22, 1776, I found myself no closer to Virginia than the day I arrived. Secrecy cloaked the flatboat operation. Colonel De Gálvez advised me to be patient, but offered no further information, except that it would leave at a minute's notice.

I kept everything packed and stacked in the corner of my room. To pass the time and earn money for the trip, I worked as a scribe for an export-import house, filling out invoices, checking incoming cargoes against their bills of lading, and serving as translator between English-speaking crews and Spanish customs officials.

At the colonel's insistence, I occupied his spare bedroom. Even so, I rarely saw him. Colonel De Gálvez came home only to sleep, change clothes, or grab a quick meal. When military duty didn't consume his time, the thirty-year-old bachelor courted the Widow De Saint Maxent.

Lieutenant Calderón proved amazingly cooperative. After my release, he handed over Papá's medical bag, my haversack, my musket, and other possessions lost my first night in New Orleans. For my part, I was grateful he had kept them for me and overjoyed to find Papá's letter to my grandfather with the seal unbroken.

Waiting for Gibson's flatboat flotilla to set out wore my patience thin, but it also had its positive side. Every night after work I headed to the Widow de Saint Maxent's house to visit Eugenie. Sometimes we played cards. Sometimes we strolled through town and talked. Other times, we attended a dance. New Orleans loved parties.

Every night someone hosted a ball.

Tonight, Eugenie and I were on our way to the British ambassador's house. It was a British holiday, the King's Coronation Day. I'd bought the fanciest clothes I'd ever owned, just for the ball. In black satin knee breeches with golden buckles, white silk stockings and shirt, an embroidered waistcoat, and double-breasted jacket covered with large gilt buttons, I felt like a gentleman from head to toe.

At the stroke of seven, we entered the British ambassador's ballroom. I bowed while Eugenie curtseyed to the ambassador, a gray, thin-faced man who greeted her warmly.

"How beautiful you look tonight," he told her.

In a floor-length sea-green gown that showed off her fair skin and luminous green eyes, she was the prettiest girl in the room. Pearl-encrusted combs held her reddish-gold hair in a twist. Her skirts rustled like wind through tree branches. On her arm she carried a large, white-beaded drawstring purse.

"Milord," she said, "may I present Mr. Bannister."

For one heart-stopping moment, I thought he would refuse to admit me because of my fight with Saber-Scar and his other embassy guards, but he acknowledged me with a quick nod, as if I were no more significant than the insects buzzing around sconces bolted to the wall. He directed all his attention to Eugenie. "You must save me a dance."

"It would be an honor, Milord," she replied.

At Eugenie's suggestion, we headed to a dark corner at the back of the room and settled onto a sofa across from fifteen-foot-high doors framed by crimson drapes. To our left, a row of chairs marched toward the entryway.

She leaned toward me and spoke in French, then lifted an eyebrow as if she expected an answer.

"I don't speak French. Remember?"

"*Dommage, mon petit chou,*" she clucked.

I squinted at her. "What does that mean?"

She wagged her finger. "It means you must learn French."

"For you, Eugenie, I would learn a thousand languages." Embarrassment exploded through me. I avoided her eyes. Why had I said such a silly thing?

"That is very sweet." She stretched toward me and gave me a peck on the cheek.

My temperature climbed. I took her warm, soft hand and gently kissed it.

"I will miss you when you go to Virginia," she said.

"I'll miss you, too."

The Spanish had imposed their laws and their money on New Orleans, but little else. The city refused to give up its French customs, language, and traditions. I could understand why. French was a beautiful language, as beautiful as its women.

I suddenly recalled something Papá had said on our trip from Saltillo to San Antonio. He had just received a letter from my grandfather in Virginia, and we were on our way back east so the two of them could patch up their differences.

"Julia's a nice girl," Papá remarked in an offhand manner as he tied his horse to a mesquite tree. "You can write her when we get to Virginia. I'm sure she'll be glad to hear from you."

I pulled my hat brim a little lower to hide my embarrassment. When did Papá figure out I liked Julia?

Papá had a sly look about him, but said not a word more. He went to his saddlebag and drew out our lunch of hardtack and *carne seca*, the dried meat Indians called *charqui*.

The Texas sun beat down insufferably hot, making me appreciate the mesquite's shade.

"Your mother was about Julia's age when we married."

Another supposedly offhand remark.

Papá took a bite of the *charqui* and chewed for several seconds. "She was seventeen years old."

I had always been curious about my mother, who had died from complications in childbirth when my little brother was stillborn. Certain things I knew from simple logic. Papá was tall and blond with large gray-green eyes, but my hair and eyes were as black as black could be. My light copper skin suggested my mother was dark. The only feature I inherited from Papá was his coarse, straight hair.

"How did you and Mamá meet?"

His eyes took on a faraway look, as if he could see all the way to his childhood home in Virginia. "One day, a Mexican gentleman visited my father's plantation on business. Something to do with buying tobacco. I returned from fox hunting in time to watch him and your future mother alight from their carriage. She was the most beautiful woman I had ever laid eyes on. The moment I saw her, I knew I was in love."

I leaned forward, deeply interested. "It was love at first sight?"

Papá gave me a cockeyed grin. "When Bannister men fall in love, they fall hard. They say Cupid shoots you with an arrow. 'Tisn't so. He throws a piece of hardtack at you and knocks you senseless."

"I'm never going to fall in love," I bragged. Just in time, I dodged a piece of hardtack Papá threw at me.

"Famous last words, son. Famous last words."

Now, as I gazed at Eugenie, my heart lurched, and I felt like I'd been hit in the head with a piece of hardtack. It saddened me to think of leaving Eugenie, but I was anxious for the flatboat trip to begin so I could deliver my father's letter.

Eugenie gestured toward the ambassador's receiving line. "Look who's here."

Captain Gibson had just walked into the room. I stared at him in shock. An American rebel at the British ambassador's ball. There would be fireworks tonight.

Chapter Seven

The ambassador paled with surprise, then flushed with anger. He and Gibson exchanged stares, like two strange dogs sizing each other up. Although I sat too far away to catch a word of their conversation, I could read Gibson's smug expression as he thrust an invitation under the ambassador's nose. How did Gibson come by an invitation? He obviously wasn't on the guest list. After a short discussion punctuated by angry hand gestures, the ambassador admitted him in order to avoid a disturbance.

For the first time since we'd met, I saw Gibson in something other than buckskin and moccasins. He moved with an aristocratic bearing, as if long accustomed to his silk shirt, embroidered waistcoat, satin knee breeches, and matching jacket.

I stared in amazement and whispered to Eugenie, "I've never seen Captain Gibson look so . . . so . . . "

"Elegant? His grandmother was the daughter of a French count. She married a Pennsylvania miller."

Gibson worked his way around the room, speaking to every single person. Faces brightened at his approach. Eventually, he came toward us, a cigar in one hand and a champagne glass in the other.

I stood, as I always did in the presence of my seniors, but Eugenie remained seated, as was the custom.

"Good to see you again, Gator. You've come up in the world."

He grinned as he rubbed my lapel between his fingers.

Next, he bent over Eugenie's hand. "Such loveliness can only leave a trail of broken hearts. Mine, among them." Saying that, Gibson straightened and winked at her.

"Why, Captain Gibson. If I didn't know better, I'd think you were flirting with me."

He grinned. "Me? Flirt? My mother did not bear a foolish son. I've seen Gator fight. I know better than to flirt with his girl."

A little later, the ambassador approached and escorted Eugenie onto the dance floor. He ignored me, as before, but looked at Gibson with evident distaste.

Gibson, in a typical display of good humor, smiled and saluted him with his cigar.

When they were out of earshot, I asked, "When do we leave, sir?"

"Excellent question. I've been wondering that myself. I wish to be home by Christmas. I have a newborn son I've never seen." He exhaled a long plume of smoke. "Colonel De Gálvez assures me it won't be long now."

"If we don't leave soon, the Ohio will be frozen over, and we won't reach Fort Pitt until spring."

"Patience isn't your strong suit, Gator." Captain Gibson squashed out his cigar in a ceramic bowl. "Mine neither. Washington's soldiers are dying from smallpox. How many will perish before we return? The medicine does no good gathering dust in Colonel De Gálvez's warehouse. General Washington needs that quinine desperately. He can't afford to lose any more troops. He's running dangerously low on gunpowder, and bullets as well. Some of his soldiers don't even have muskets. Some are barefoot!"

"Aren't the British ambassador and his spies growing suspicious?"

"Yes. Daily it becomes harder and harder to explain why I and my so-called fur traders haven't returned to Pennsylvania."

"Then why are you here, flaunting your presence? I mean, the ambassador's ball was the last place I expected you to be."

"Last place I expected to be, as well. The colonel has a plan. All I know is he told Eugenie to visit the British ambassador and steal an invitation . . ."

"What?" I felt blood drain from my face.

"Dear boy, didn't you know she's a reformed thief?"

My heart hammered. No one had told me that. I somehow managed to shake my head.

"Soon after Colonel De Gálvez came to Louisiana, he arrested Eugenie for thievery. When he learned she had lost her entire family to yellow fever several months earlier and had been living on the streets, he decided to help her rather than punish her. The colonel believes we should give our heart to God and our hand to man. He found her a position as the Widow De Saint Maxent's personal maid."

I watched Eugenie on the dance floor. What a miserable life she must have led, living in tatters, foraging through trash, sleeping on the streets. I recalled how scared and alone I felt after Papá died.

The hours crept by. Man after man asked Eugenie to dance. She never refused, but she always complained about the heat in the ballroom upon her return and dipped into her drawstring purse for a handkerchief to delicately mop her forehead and bosom.

At eleven-thirty on the dot, I watched Captain Gibson navigate around clusters of guests. When he was three feet away, he bowed low to Eugenie, then me. "May I have your permission to dance with Miss Dubreton?"

I wanted to refuse so Eugenie and I could continue our conversation, but knew I could not. My eyes never left them as they glided around the room to a quick violin melody. Toward the end of the piece, Eugenie missed a step and stumbled into him. Red-faced, she clung to Gibson's dark blue jacket a moment, patted his chest, and smoothed his lapels.

She must be tired, I said to myself. She's been dancing all night.

The complete gentleman, Captain Gibson brought her back. Following etiquette scrupulously, he thanked us and returned to his seat.

Less than thirty minutes later, the bells of the parish church chimed midnight. As if on cue, Colonel De Gálvez and six musketed infantrymen marched into the ambassador's ballroom. As they entered, the music faded and the dancers, rumbling with discontent, splintered to let the soldiers through.

Colonel De Gálvez and his entourage tramped over to Captain Gibson and formed a semicircle around him.

"George Gibson," Colonel De Gálvez said in a voice loud enough for everyone to hear, "you are under arrest."

Chapter Eight

Everyone gasped, except the British ambassador who smiled smugly at the turn of events.

Captain Gibson took a sip of champagne and regarded Colonel De Gálvez through narrowed eyes. "The devil I am. As an officer in the Continental Army, I deserve . . ."

"You are a rebel," the British ambassador interjected, "and a traitor to your country. You deserve to hang."

At a nod from Colonel De Gálvez, soldiers grabbed Gibson by the arms and hauled him from his chair.

Gibson's eyes were large and bright with anger. "What is the meaning of this? Colonel De Gálvez, I thought the Spanish were neutral."

"Search him," De Gálvez ordered.

Two soldiers rifled through Gibson's pockets. They extracted several leather pocketbooks, the kind men used to carry money and traveling documents. Colonel De Gálvez flourished the stolen items overhead. Mouth agape, Gibson froze. In unison, he and I darted a look at Eugenie. She must have planted the stolen items on Gibson during their dance. But why? At least now I knew she'd carried that oversized purse to conceal the wallets she had stolen.

"Take this 'American' nobody away," Colonel De Gálvez ordered with a scornful flick of the wrist.

Horrified, I watched soldiers usher Captain Gibson from the ballroom at bayonet point.

My head spun with confusion. I rose unsteadily and

took a step toward Colonel De Gálvez, but stopped short. His large, black eyes held a hard, flinty look I'd never seen before.

Eugenie tugged on my sleeve. "*Mon cher*, Colonel De Gálvez has just cause to arrest Gibson. Trust me."

How could I? This made no sense. I fell into an empty chair along the far wall. The world had come crashing down around me. What was I to do now? Was I ever going to get to Virginia?

Interest in Gibson's arrest and speculation about what it meant soon waned and the dancing resumed.

Eugenie slipped her hand in mine. "Come."

"Eugenie!" I protested, my mind unable to absorb all that had just happened. "I do not wish to dance."

"Come," she insisted.

Instead of leading me to the dance floor, she guided me toward the back door. She glanced nervously over her shoulder and appeared relieved no one noticed our imminent departure.

Halfway down the exterior staircase, a chill went through me, for in the street below stood Calderón, pistol in hand. Instead of his usual impeccable uniform, he wore a black full-sleeve shirt, black trousers, and knee boots. His hair hung in stringy, wet locks on both sides of his mud-smudged face.

Eugenie urged me down the stairs, toward him.

Calderón smiled at her and tipped his hat, then scowled the way he always did when he saw me. "By Colonel De Gálvez's command, you are to come with me."

"Where to?"

"I am not at liberty to say!" he replied curtly.

"Trust us," Eugenie said. "He is only following orders. We are to take you to Colonel De Gálvez. That's all I can tell you."

I didn't like the sound of that, but I knew a soldier's honor was as sacred as a woman's virtue. If Calderón was acting on orders, nothing I could say or do would convince him to release me. My spirits sank a little lower.

With Eugenie in the lead, me in the center, and Calderón at my back, we moved silently through the city streets. Instead of heading for the jail, where I expected to join Captain Gibson, they took me in the opposite direction, northward, toward the swamps.

My mind searched frantically for answers. Where were we going? Why the secrecy? Why couldn't they tell me something, anything?

In spite of her ball gown, Eugenie bunched her skirt in her hands and set a brisk pace through the shadowy streets, toward the upper portion of New Orleans. Once in a while, she glanced over her shoulder. Leaving the city, she charged down a twisting path carved out by wild animals, through tangled undergrowth, unbothered by briars and vines that flogged our faces. She seemed to know every tree root, stump, and rock along the way.

When we halted under cypresses festooned with curtains of gray Spanish moss, Calderón squatted and yanked me down beside him to the damp, spongy ground. He cocked his head, as if listening for something. The sound of pursuers? A signal? Eugenie tucked her mud-splattered gown around her. Crickets and frogs chorused together in the dark. I slapped at a mosquito buzzing by my ear.

"Stay still," Calderón growled.

"Eugenie," I whispered, ignoring him, "what . . .?"

Calderón silenced me with a fierce "Shut up."

Wisps of cloud swirled over a golden sliver of moon. Little breezes played from one tree to another. The swamp smelled of decaying vegetation and wet peat moss. An owl hooted. Calderón cupped his hand to his mouth and hooted twice.

"Who-o-o! Who-o-o! Who-o-o!" came the swift reply. A signal.

Calderón and Eugenie smiled at each other and jumped up at the same time. We scrambled down a steep riverbank, slipping and sliding in a hail of loose rocks and dirt. Below us, moonlight danced off the Mississippi. And bobbing in the ripples . . .

My God. I stopped suddenly, and Calderón plowed into me.

Flatboats!

Chapter Nine

"Halt and be recognized!" A sentinel swung toward us, his musket leveled.

By instinct, we raised our hands.

"We are people of peace," Calderón said in a voice that showed no fear.

The sentinel stepped aside and peered anxiously into the dark forest for signs we'd been followed.

Three flatboats were tied to trees lining the riverbank. Two canoes rode beside them. Buckskinned men in coonskin caps scurried about in the dark, toting crates and barrels and gunny sacks while musketed men stood guard on shore.

Each flatboat looked like a floating house about fifty feet long, rectangular, and with a cabin in the center. At the bow was a small-caliber cannon that could swivel in any direction.

Calderón walked up to Colonel De Gálvez, who stood with his back to us. "Your Excellency. Mr. Bannister is here."

Colonel De Gálvez turned and grinned. "Good work, Lieutenant." He bestowed a fatherly kiss on Eugenie's forehead. "Congratulations. You did it."

She angled her head to the right. "Did you have any doubts?"

Colonel De Gálvez laughed. "I'd rather not answer that question."

A man waved frantically to me from the cabin's curved roof and clambered down a six-rung ladder. In one swift motion, he swung himself over the side and leaped to shore.

It was Lieutenant William Linn, Gibson's second-in-command. As usual, he wore a puffy-sleeved shirt and homespun trousers held up by suspenders.

I turned to Colonel De Gálvez in confusion. "I don't understand. Why did you arrest Captain Gibson? Isn't he going with us?"

Colonel De Gálvez put his hands on my shoulders. "Lorenzo, I apologize for the deception. To keep the British ambassador in the dark, no one, except myself, Eugenie, and Lt. Calderón knew our plans."

"Not even Captain Gibson?"

"He knew he would be arrested," Eugenie said, "but he didn't know when or on what charges."

"No one knew the details of the plan," Colonel De Gálvez said. "That way everyone would react naturally when it happened. Gibson will remain in my jail until the flatboats are safely away. When the time is right, I shall put Gibson on the next ship heading north—without the British ambassador's knowledge."

Frowning at Eugenie, I said, "You planted those pocketbooks on him while you were dancing."

"Indeed I did, *mon petit chou.*"

I had been watching closely and missed it. But then, I'd been keeping an eye on Eugenie's dancing partners for misconduct. Not her.

Colonel De Gálvez drew me and Calderón away from the others. "Lt. Calderón is the special envoy sent by King Carlos to make certain the supplies reach the Americans. I have assigned him the additional duty of escorting you on a particular service. I wish you to deliver a letter."

He handed me a sealed envelope. "Give this to His Excellency, General George Washington, commander in chief of the Continental Army."

My eyes rounded and my heart skipped a beat. "I am

honored, Colonel." Oddly, it bore no address. I looked at the colonel questioningly.

"The letter is written in disappearing ink for reasons of security," the colonel said. "Lieutenant Calderón knows the formula to make the ink reappear. The two of you must deliver the letter together. General Washington does not speak Spanish. I do not speak English, nor does Lieutenant Calderón. You will translate the letter for the general. Lieutenant Calderón will see you to the general's camp."

"By your leave, Your Excellency," Calderón said, solemn-faced, "I shall show Mr. Bannister to his quarters." He led me toward the largest flatboat.

We scrambled across a narrow board that served as a gangplank and jumped to the rough cypress planking. The flatboat listed under our added weight.

In the cabin, Calderón lit a lantern hanging from a peg. The cabin resembled a little house with a small shuttered window on each wall, two comfortable bunks, a fireplace, table and chairs.

I inhaled sharply. All my worldly treasures were there, and more to boot. Papá's medical bag, my musket, my haversack. Lined up on a shelf along the wall were little alabaster jars of unguents, pigments, and creams. Peruvian bark, calomel, opium, all expensive drugs. When I opened my father's medical bag, I found everything as he had left it. Forceps for extracting bullets, scalpels, bandages, tourniquets, sponges, amputating instruments. A small shelf held a medical library. *Gerald's Herbal* and *Plain Concise Practical Remarks on the Treatment of Wounds and Fractures* by Dr. John Jones. On the fly page, Colonel De Gálvez had written in an elegant hand, "May God watch over you. I pray these books prove an enlightening, but unnecessary addition to your journey."

I slipped the colonel's letter to General Washington between the pages of *Gerald's Herbal* and eased the book shut, careful not to let any of the letter show.

I undressed and hung my party clothes on pegs around the walls. "See here, Lieutenant," I said as I pulled a deerskin hunting shirt over my head, "we're about the same age. Calling me 'Mr. Bannister' seems foolish."

"On the contrary. It is the height of wisdom."

"What do you mean?" I pulled up leather breeches.

He looked at me as if he had greatly underestimated my ignorance. "Considering your age, the men need to call you 'Mister' as a reminder to show you the proper respect. Furthermore, it's the proper address for the medical officer on a ship. This is an important mission. It must succeed. The consequences, should I fail, are enormous. If we are discovered, Spain will be dragged into the war prematurely. We are not yet ready to take on Britain. The rebels need supplies, and without them, they will lose the war."

"Yes. I understand all that."

"Failure also means my military career is over. From Colonel De Gálvez's mouth to the king's ear."

"You must be joking."

Giving me an amazed stare, he said, "Colonel De Gálvez comes from the most influential family in Spain. Did you truly not know that? His uncle is José De Gálvez, minister of the Indies, second only to the king. If we are attacked at any time during our trip, do me a favor and take cover. I have to deliver you in a whole skin."

"Alive, I presume?"

"That would be the best for both of us," Calderón said grimly. "If the British capture us and find that letter to General Washington," he said, nodding toward *Gerald's Herbal*, "you and I will hang as spies."

Chapter Ten

Calderón and I returned ashore and hurried toward Colonel De Gálvez and Eugenie, who were still waiting patiently.

The colonel's eyes were sad. "I am sorry to see you go, Lorenzo." He pulled me to him in a Spanish-style embrace, then pushed back. "No one place is better than another. If your heart is right, you can be happy anywhere."

"I hope everything works out with your grandfather," Eugenie said. "If it doesn't, you can always come back here."

My hand found hers and gave it a gentle squeeze. "Some day I'll return to New Orleans."

She returned my squeeze.

"When you reach Fort Pitt," the colonel said, "Lt. Linn will give you a chit to present to the Continental Congress. It will entitle you to twenty-five dollars a month for your services as medic."

"Twenty-five dollars?" It was more than I earned as a scribe, and it was twice a second lieutenant's salary. I didn't know what to say. "Thank you, Your Excellency."

"Don't thank me. The Continental Congress thought this mission so important they gave Gibson and Linn a generous letter of credit that authorizes them to obtain money or necessities for them and their men. You are one of those necessities. If you will excuse me," he said, a ghost of a smile on his lips. He darted an understanding look at Eugenie and drifted away.

"So you're going," she said. Tears filled her eyes.

I nodded. My throat squeezed so tight, I couldn't answer. A month ago, I didn't even know she existed, and now I didn't want to leave her.

"All hands on board." Calderón headed toward the head flatboat. "Platoon One to the oars." He climbed a six-rung ladder to the cabin roof to man a long-handled oar secured in an oarlock.

Two Spanish soldiers with muskets at the ready stood at the bow amid huge barrels while other men set oars in the locks.

I lowered my face slowly and kissed Eugenie's lips. They tasted like strawberries. My temperature shot up ten degrees.

"Mr. Bannister!" Calderón called out in a faintly impatient voice. "If you please."

"Au revoir, Eugenie."

"Au revoir, mon petit chou."

I climbed into the flatboat. Spanish soldiers loosened the ropes and gave the flatboats a hard shove. I waved to Eugenie and she waved back. The day I'd looked forward to for so long had finally arrived, but as I watched Eugenie grow smaller and smaller, I realized New Orleans was a city I could learn to love. Leaving her behind left me with a sense of loss.

The flatboats turned the first bend in the river and she disappeared from view.

Chapter Eleven

Too excited to sleep, I sat on deck and watched the rowers—silent, serious, shirtless—work their oars. It took all their strength to move the flatboats upstream against a strong current. Veins in their necks stood out from the effort. The Spaniards and Americans manning the twenty oarlocks port and starboard had arms as thick as tree trunks. Gibson had chosen his men for their incredible strength, as had Colonel De Gálvez.

Although sails were hoisted, they hung as limp as the Spanish flag off our stern. A wall of trees along the river-bank prevented a breeze from catching in our sails and helping our boat upstream.

The men rowed with swift, strong strokes. They bent and pulled, bent and pulled. Cypress and orange trees slid past.

"Can't sleep?" a whispered voice asked. William Linn flopped down beside me on the rough planking. "Me neither."

I heard an alligator snort in a bayou far away and hoped he would stay where he was.

In the dark, about three hundred yards ahead, lanterns swinging right and left sent light dancing over the water.

I moved forward for a closer look. "What are they doing?" I asked, pointing to the canoes.

"The Mississippi is always low this time of year. That means our lookouts must keep a sharp eye for sunken trees, sandbanks, shoals, islands. Normally, our scouts call out steering directions so the pilots can navigate around them. But sound travels well across the water. We are under orders to make no loud or unnecessary noises."

"Why must everyone be so quiet?"

"We slipped out of New Orleans without the British ambassador's knowledge. If he finds out we've left, he'll alert British forts along the way. I like my hair and I'd like to keep it."

Confused by his statement, I twisted toward him.

"The British give the Indians guns and whiskey for Yankee scalps. Men, women, children. It doesn't matter to the British." William shook his head. "Buying the scalps of fellow British citizens doesn't seem to bother them."

I grimaced. What did a scalp look like? Was there dried blood on it? A sickening smell? What did it feel like to touch one?

William fingered a lock of his pale yellow hair. "The Indians are especially fond of unusual-colored hair."

I thought about Eugenie's long, reddish-gold tresses.

"Shame Captain Gibson isn't here. He knows all about scalps. He speaks a dozen or so Indian dialects like a native." William chuckled. "The Gibsons could charm the skin off a snake. Must be in their blood. Gibson's brother John was captured by the Indians. They killed his companions but an Indian woman rescued him Pocahontas-style. If I could bottle the Gibson charm, I'd sell it and become a rich man."

I struggled to hold back a laugh.

Grinning, William raised his hand, as if taking an oath. "Captain Gibson is part French nobility. That's why he speaks French and Spanish and has those fancy airs. Now, my family doesn't have a drop of noble blood. My great-grandfather came here from Ireland as an indentured servant. My father is a blacksmith."

A movement to my right caught my eye.

Calderón picked his way among the sleeping men on deck. He bent down, tapped them one by one on the arm, and jerked his thumb toward the oars.

Like spirits rising from the tomb, they got up and shuffled toward the side of the boat. The exhausted oarsmen they replaced stretched out at my feet and were soon fast asleep.

William laced his hands behind his head. "My father wants me to take up a profession, instead of tramping through the woods. Thinks I'll wander off on another trip with Dan'l Boone and get myself killed. When the war's over, I'm going to settle in Kentucky. Kentucky." He said the name with great fondness. "Now there's the place to be. More game than you can shake a stick at. Buffalo, deer, turkey."

Calderón looked my way and gave me a sympathetic smile that seemed to say, "That man will talk your ear off."

We continued upstream in this manner for another hour. Other than William's lowered voice, the only sound was the stroking of the oars against the water and the grind of wood in the oarlocks.

A few hours later, Calderón raised his voice over the rush of water. "Strip your oars. Odd men first."

Every other rower removed strips of cloth that had been wrapped around the oars to muffle the sound. That operation finished, I gathered the cloth and laid it out on deck to dry. Given the hot night air, it didn't take long. I folded them neatly into a pile and took them to the cabin.

"Our Father, who art in heaven," I silently prayed, "let me never need them as bandages."

Chapter Twelve

"Ursula Major. Ursula Minor. Orion." I lolled back on the cabin roof, looking up at the constellations. From my vantage point, I could see rowers on both sides of the boat. They had worked the oars night and day. Sweat ran off them in rivulets.

We were making good time. Twenty-four hours after leaving New Orleans, we were fifty miles north of the city.

Feeling as useless as wet gunpowder, I decided it was time to water the Lambs again.

At first I merely put the dipper to their lips so they could drink without breaking the rhythm of the oars. On a whim, I poured water over Corporal García's head to help him cool off. He shut his eyes tight and laughed, but never missed a stroke. "Thanks, Mr. Bannister. That felt good."

"Watch out," a man called out as I drew near. "Here comes John the Baptist." He bent his head to accept the refreshing water.

"Hey, Baptizer," Red called out. "My stomach is rubbing against my backbone. Can you fetch me some hardtack?"

"What's the point?" I shot back with a grin. "You'll just get hungry again."

Laughter rippled up and down the side of the boat.

No sooner had I finished watering the Lambs than a new problem presented itself. We rowed straight into clouds of mosquitoes. They lit on arms and necks and backs and produced monstrous welts. Between slapping at the insects and scratching bites, an idea sprang to mind. I slipped into the cabin and took a tin of cooking grease from the shelf. I added charcoal and soot from the fireplace to make an ointment that I offered the men. They dipped their hands into the tin and smeared gobs of grease all over them.

Calderón frowned at me and for a moment I thought he would reprimand me for misuse of cooking grease. Instead, a smile erased his scowl. "Thank you, Mister Bannister," he said loud enough for everyone to hear. "I admire a man with initiative and foresight."

William wrinkled his nose in disgust at the strong, disagreeable odor, until he saw no one else but him scratching and slapping at mosquitoes.

Hours and hours went by. A wave of sleepiness rolled over me. I squeezed myself into a tight ball on the fore-deck beside a canvas-covered box of muskets and shut my eyes. I dreamed I was back in San Antonio on that fatal evening, August 7, 1776.

⁂ ⁂ ⁂

Stiff from riding, I swung down from my horse and led her toward the stable, leaving my fellow ranch hands by the corral gate discussing how to spend their weekly earnings. As I unbuckled the cinch, I heard the hurried slap-slap of sandals on the sun-baked ground. I turned.

A monk from the mission trotted toward me, his brown robes snapping in the breeze. "Lorenzo! Come quick. Your father is dying."

My insides turned to water. Resting my forehead against the leather saddle, I tried to absorb the words. For months I'd watched the slow progress of Papá's disease. I'd had time to prepare for Papá's death, but I couldn't accept it.

The monk's voice brought me out of my stupor. "I'll take care of your horse. Go to your father."

I nodded and mumbled my thanks. Head spinning, I dashed from the stable, through the mission patio, into the tiled hallway. Tears blurred my vision. I paused in the doorway of our room and wiped my eyes. Gathering my courage, I focused on the labored rise and fall of Papá's chest. Wordless, the monk by Papá's bedside rose and left. Nothing had changed since I had checked on Papá at noon. His lunch rested on the night stand untouched. Our meager baggage remained piled in one corner, as if we were ready to take flight at a moment's notice.

To keep from pacing around in circles, I eased into a chair beside Papá's bed, took his pulse, and wiped his forehead with a cool cloth. Not knowing what else to do, I picked up a medical book. For the thousandth time, I flipped it open and read the description and treatment for consumption. I searched for something, anything, to help Papá. A new treatment. A promising drug. Day after day, night after night, Papá suffered. I would have done anything to save him, but consumption had no cure. A numbing sense of defeat settled over me.

The bugle called all mission soldiers to evening parade. I leaned forward in the cane-bottomed chair beside Papá's bed and took his pulse. It grew weaker by the hour. Papá was slipping away.

A sob welled up inside me, but I forced it down. He expected me to be brave. To hide my tears, I poured water into a tin basin and scrubbed caked-on dirt from my face. After a day of riding herd on longhorn cattle, I smelled of horse sweat and worse. I still wore mud-splattered chaps, dusty boots, and a flannel shirt.

I fished out five Spanish pillar dollars, my weekly salary as a ranch hand, and stared at the gold coins in my hand. Five Spanish pillar dollars. Our money had run out long ago. I hid the truth from Papá. He didn't know we were living on the monks' charity, although he probably suspected our financial situation was bleak.

God bless the ranch foreman who had suspected my financial situation and had given me a job. Plus, work took my mind off Papá's condition.

Through the open window, I watched fifty or so soldiers with muskets and bayonets muster on the central plaza of the mission. In my head, I went through the manual of arms with them. "Port arms! Shoulder arms! Right face! March!" How I longed to be a soldier guarding Spanish missions and forts in the Province of Texas and protecting settlers from marauding Indians.

Papá let out a long, ragged cough. I took his hand. His skin felt paper-thin. Pale, propped up by a half dozen pillows, he looked fragile. Dark circles ringed his eyes. "Lorenzo," Papá said, his voice barely a whisper. "What is the fascination with muskets and bayonets?"

For as long as I could remember, Papá worked as a civilian doctor for the Spanish army. I grew up around the military. Maybe that explained the excitement that surged through me whenever I heard the bugle call or saw soldiers in colorful uniforms.

"Papá, why didn't you join the military?"

"I don't like to take orders. Your grandfather . . . " He paused to take a breath. " . . . wanted me to join the British navy. I wanted to be a doctor."

"Is that why you all quarreled?"

Papá's gaze held mine. "No. It was because of your mother. He didn't want me to have a relationship with 'a woman beneath my station,' as he put it."

Papá put a blood-flecked handkerchief to his lips and coughed. For a long time, he hid his condition from me. Then one day, three months ago, he spit up blood and I realized he was dying of consumption.

"I was right to take you and your mother from Virginia." He rested a moment. "My father has finally recognized that."

My eyes roved to a note wedged between two candlesticks on the night stand. "Come home, Jack," my grandfather had written, "and we will work out the differences between us."

Papá gestured toward a sealed envelope addressed to my grandfather. "I dictated a letter to a monk while you were gone. This letter is important, Lorenzo. Promise me you will deliver it."

"Upon my word of honor . . ."

⟨⟩ ⟨⟩ ⟨⟩

The slap of a hand against the cabin wall jolted me awake.

"All hands up and at their oars," Calderón ordered.

Men stumbled up from the rough floorboards where they had spent the night with no more room than a man in his coffin. They stretched. Yawned. Squinted against the morning glare. Scratched themselves. Relieved themselves over the boat edge.

I pretended to rub the sleep from my eyes, but in reality I was wiping away tears. My chest throbbed with pain whenever I thought about Papá. How I missed him. I looked up at flights of waterfowl slicing the morning fog. Pink clouds appeared over twisted cypress trees bordering the river. I bounded up and headed toward the narrow footwalk that ran the length of the boat on both sides. Staying busy always helped ease the pain.

"Where do you think you're going?" Calderón asked, stepping in front of me.

"I'm going to row."

"You are our physician."

"So? It's my turn . . ."

"No."

"I've never taken a turn at the oars, and these men have been rowing . . ."

"Enough." Calderón drew his finger across his neck in a quick slicing motion. "In the cabin, please."

Reluctantly, I complied.

Calderón closed the door behind him and turned to face me. "First. Don't argue with me in front of the men. It's bad form. Second. I am in command here and you will obey me. Third. The physician on board always enjoys the prerogatives of officers, and no officer takes to the oars."

"I don't like the idea of special privileges."

"You are educated and hold privileges over your elders who are not."

"I just wanted to help the men."

Calderón held my gaze, his face expressionless. After a long moment, he picked up an amber-colored bottle, examined it, then gave me a sidelong look. He put the bottle back, squinted at another bottle, neatly labeled in black ink, then shot me a questioning look. "Your father taught you what all this is for?"

"Yes," I said.

"The flotilla has sixteen Spaniards, fifteen Americans, but only one physician."

"Do you really expect me to sit around and twiddle my thumbs while others work?"

Calderón slapped his hands to his sides in exasperation. "Yes! Because I want all your thumbs and fingers capable of surgery should my men fall wounded."

I pulled my lips back in a tight line. "I get your point."

"About time." Calderón gestured toward the door, signaling I was dismissed.

I tried to think of an appropriate reply, but failed, so I whirled around and marched away, feeling like a child leaving the woodshed.

The Mississippi stretched a mile and a half from shore to shore. Waves slapped gently against the flatboat and helped calm me. Now and then a piece of driftwood thumped against the bow. Sunlight glittered on the looping ribbon of water ahead of us. At the corner of each flatboat stood guards combing the forest with nervous eyes.

Calderón was right. The men depended on my skill as a surgeon. I did not want to let them down.

A faint shape half-hidden behind the trees stood along the riverbank. I borrowed a telescope from one of the guardsmen, raised it, and saw a vague figure, about a half-mile away. "Lieutenant," I said in a level voice. I jerked my head toward the bronze-colored man in a buckskin breechcloth, moccasins, and leggings.

Calderón scanned the shore with his own spyglass. "Choctaw," he said.

The flatboat navigated around a turn in the river, and the Choctaw warrior was lost from view.

ZZZZ! Thud!

Something whistled past my ear and buried itself in the cabin wall. I dropped to the deck, as did everyone around me. I looked up to find an arrow in the cabin wall two inches from where I had stood.

Chapter Thirteen

More arrows whirred past and embedded themselves in the wall. Indians bolted from behind a curtain of trees and raced towards us, attacking us at the bend in the river, when the canoes and flatboats were closest to shore.

Alarm scurried down my spine. I saw a flash of scarlet. At least one British soldier, a tall man about the size of Saber-Scar, was with them.

"Musketeers! Starboard!" Calderón's voice rang with a note of command.

Soldiers lined the decks fore and aft and primed their muskets. Only four soldiers. Against how many Choctaws?

Calderón snatched up his weapon and joined them. "Ready! Aim! Fire!"

A withering volley of flame and smoke exploded across the water.

"Reload!"

His soldiers followed orders with drilled precision and waited for the smoke to clear.

"Keep rowing!" Calderón bellowed to the frightened oarsmen who had broken rhythm and were allowing the boat to drift. "Pull to port."

I realized Calderón was snapping out orders in Spanish to men who spoke only English. I translated, but added, "Lt. Calderón is giving you cover with musket smoke."

Twenty pairs of arms strained to turn the flatboat toward the left bank.

Little by little the gun smoke obscuring our view of the Choctaws cleared. Arrows whistled by, followed quickly by a salvo of gunfire. A flaming arrow buried itself in the roof. William dashed up the ladder, pulled out the arrow with a gasp of pain, and threw it into the Mississippi.

If a spark ignited the canvas-covered gunpowder, it would blow us beyond tomorrow. In one swift move, I grabbed a leather bucket filled with water, and doused the canvas.

"Lorenzo! Get inside!" Calderón grabbed me by the scruff of the neck and propelled me past the cannon two men were loading. He shoved me through the cabin door. "Stay here. Get ready."

I opened Papá's medical bag and arranged his instruments on a clean cloth. Outside the cabin's eight-inch-thick oak walls, I heard someone cry out in agony. Muskets popped.

Two men came in and deposited Corporal García on a bunk. I cut away his shirt. A gaping gunshot wound exposed his intestines. Nausea gripped me as I applied bandages in a futile attempt to save his life. I gave him a dose of opium for the pain and said a silent prayer. Within minutes I closed his eyes and covered him with a sheet.

Our cannon thundered, making the boat rock.

The door banged open. Calderón staggered in, his hand to his shoulder. I grabbed him before he collapsed and led him to an empty bunk. He took his hands away from the holes in his jacket. Dark red patches about three inches below the shoulder grew larger as I examined his wound. I placed bandages very gently inside Calderón's jacket over the blood in front and back. "That should hold the flow. Take it easy, Calderón. Keep your left arm tight across your chest."

More cannon fire. I grabbed the edge of the bunk to steady myself.

Calderón's gaze fixed on the sheet-covered form on

the opposite bunk, then turned back to me with a questioning look.

"Corporal García's gone," I said gently.

Calderón lowered his head. "He was a good soldier."

I cut away Calderón's jacket and washed the wounds with water and a clean cloth. My stomach churned. The entrance wound was a small, neat circle just below the shoulder bone. The bullet had exited in a star-shaped explosion about the size of a Spanish pillar dollar.

Beyond the cabin walls, men shouted, Indians whooped, guns banged.

"You were lucky, Calderón. It didn't hit a bone. Went clean through the flesh." He grimaced in pain when I rubbed ointment on his wound. "I know it hurts, but you're going to be fine."

Placing a rolled blanket behind him, I made him comfortable and gave him a dose of opium to ease the pain.

The door flew open. Two men carried William Linn inside and placed him on the floor. An arrow protruded from his upper thigh.

As I bent over him to treat his wound, the shooting and yelling abruptly stopped. Either we had rowed out of range or everyone outside the cabin was dead.

Chapter Fourteen

September 29: Lt. Linn's hand is badly burned. His arrow wound has confined him to bed. I have taken over his duty of recording our progress in the log book. Lt. Calderón is resting comfortably. I pray his wound does not become infected. With both Lt. Linn and Lt. Calderón wounded, I am in charge of the flatboats. A bullet grazed Red in the head, but his wound is minor. We wrapped Corporal García's body in a sail, tied a cannon ball to his ankles, and buried him in a watery grave after praying over him. The fear of another Indian attack prevented us from pulling to shore and giving him a proper burial on land.

September 30: The men are in good spirits, though exhausted and on constant alert. The threat of more attacks hangs over our head like the sword of Damocles. Calderón is running a high fever.

October 1: We are making good time. We can use the sails now, and have increased speed. Calderón's fever has broken.

October 2: The possibility that British spies in New Orleans learned of our escape worries me. I can only hope the attack three days ago was aimed at stealing our cargo, not stopping our mission.

October 3: Another 18 miles behind us.

October 6: Flatboat ran aground on a sandbar. Men pushed with oars as hard as they could until the boat swung free.

October 11: Saw two Natchez Indians on shore. They stared at us and we stared back. All quiet.

October 13: Passed Fort Rosalie, an abandoned French fort. From here on, the river becomes more treacherous. Navigating at night is now impossible. We pull to shore at dusk and make fast to trees along the bank. Anchors are useless because the soft mud on the river bottom is covered with submerged logs. Some of the men are so exhausted, they have to be carried ashore in blankets.

October 16: It is a long and difficult haul up the Mississippi. The muddiness of the river slows us, but that isn't the worst part. The river twists and turns like a snake. A distance of 100 miles measured in a straight line winds up being 180.

October 17: The farther north we travel, the clearer the Mississippi becomes. I keep ceramic crocks filled with strong, brown Mississippi water. When the water settles, a half-pint tumbler yields two inches of slime. In spite of this, the water is wholesome and tastes good. It is cool even on the hottest days. The rowers drink it down, sediment and all, and never suffer any bad effects.

October 18: Passed a British fort in broad daylight. They saw us, but did nothing. We can only speculate why.

⊰⊱ ⊰⊱ ⊰⊱

William hobbled to my writing table and read over my shoulder. "Good job, Lorenzo." He initialed the log with his uninjured hand. "I hate being wounded. I feel useless."

I cleaned the quill and put away my writing utensils. "Why do you think the British didn't attack? Are they planning something?"

"Wish I knew. Maybe they saw the Spanish flag and decided not to attack a neutral vessel, or maybe they don't know where our cargo is headed. Most likely, they see flatboats with the Spanish flag going upriver to St. Louis every week or so."

"St. Louis? Where's that?"

"Farther up the Mississippi, past the Ohio River, on the western bank. The French founded it, but the Spanish own it now."

I stretched my arms over my head, glad another long day was drawing to a close.

Calderón lay in the bunk just as I had left him, snoring, twitching, and grunting like a man with a troubled conscience.

I served myself a mug of steaming coffee. Usually, I liked my coffee laced with cream and sugar, but nowadays I took it black because I needed to stay alert. With the only two officers on board wounded, my extra responsibilities kept me occupied until well into the night. If only Captain Gibson were here.

I pulled a chair close to Calderón and sat there for a few minutes while I built up the courage to lift his dressing. My chin on my fist, I tried to figure out a mystery. Calderón reminded me of someone. My gaze fell upon his profile, particularly his nose, and then it dawned on me.

"No," I muttered. "It can't be." I took a Spanish pillar dollar from my pocket and studied it a moment.

Calderón's profile bore astounding similarities to the king's.

Suddenly, it all fit together. Calderón was related to King Carlos—probably his nephew. Colonel De Gálvez once told me Calderón had powerful friends at court. Did he mean the king himself?

I tugged gently at Calderón's bandage. Dried blood and pus made it stick to his skin. It looked bad. It smelled even worse. A sour taste came to my mouth.

Calderón's eyes slowly opened and peered up at me. "Where are we now?"

"About a week away from Fort Arkansas. If we could go as straight as a bird could fly, we'd be at the mouth of the Ohio by now." I cleaned his wound.

Calderón clenched and unclenched his jaw.

"This is nothing," I said offhandedly. "I've seen worse." I pointed to the scar over my left eyebrow that I had earned fighting Saber-Scar.

"That little scratch? I've got a rapier wound that puts it to shame." He swung his legs over the edge of the bunk and attempted to rise.

My hands on his chest, I forced him to lie back. "I believe you. You're not strong enough to get up yet, Calderón."

"Don't you think it's time you called me by my first name?"

"Which is?"

"Héctor."

"Héctor?" I nearly choked on the name. The image of a wizened old man leaped to mind, not a big-nosed lout.

"Do you find something amusing?" Calderón asked.

I didn't answer. Instead, I focused on changing his bandage. "Where on earth did you get a name like that?"

Calderón stiffened. "The king himself gave me that name."

"Are you related to King Carlos?"

"Yes," he answered in a subdued tone.

A tiny breath of moist air blew through the open window and brought a spicy smell from the forest.

"What was your father like?" Calderón asked.

My chest ached at the sudden question. I still missed Papá and didn't want to talk about him. "He was my father," I said, lifting a shoulder.

"Where's your home?"

"San Antonio . . . I guess."

"You guess? Were you born there?"

"No. I was born in Virginia."

"And you grew up in San Antonio?"

"No. Papá and I traveled around a lot."

"Where to?"

"Saltillo, Mexico City, Albuquerque, Havana."

"Sounds like you two were running from the law."

My eyes jerked up and held him. Was he making fun of me? Insulting Papá?

"My God, Lorenzo," Calderón said with the hint of a smile. "It was a joke. A feeble one, but a joke nonetheless."

Unknowingly, Calderón had touched a nerve. Sometimes I regretted our frequent moves. No sooner did I make friends than we pulled up stakes again. On the other hand, I had been lots of places, seen lots of things.

"Papá worked for the military hospital in Saltillo and often visited patients at frontier forts. His work required him to travel from fort to fort, and we never stayed more than a couple of months in one place."

"So how did you end up in San Antonio?"

"Why all the questions?"

He shrugged. "Just a way to pass the time."

"Papá was in Saltillo when he grew ill. He wrote my grandfather. I think he missed Virginia and longed to be buried in the land of his birth. Papá and my grandfather were estranged for years. My grandfather wrote back and agreed to let Papá return home. We were on our way to Virginia, but stopped in San Antonio, when Papá grew too weak to travel on. Papá is buried there." Overcome with emotion, my voice cracked.

Calderón didn't say anything for a long time. "What did your father die of?" His tone was soft.

"Consumption."

"What will you do in Virginia?"

"I'll stay with my grandfather until I'm old enough to

join the army."

"So you're going to be a medic in the army."

"No. I want to be a regular soldier."

Calderón yawned.

"Am I boring you?"

"Sorry. I'm just tired." Calderón's eyes focused on me. "Why did your father leave Virginia in the first place?"

"My grandfather didn't approve of his choice of wives. They argued. My grandfather ordered Papá off the plantation. Papá took me and my mother to New Spain when I was just a baby."

"You're going to live with a total stranger?"

I nodded. "Everyone's a stranger until you meet them." Embarrassed by all the intimate revelations, I walked outside. Late afternoon light struggled through the treetops. In an hour it would be full dark. I climbed to the roof and helped William draw in the fishing lines.

"Pull to shore," he called out. "Time for supper." As usual, a shout of "hallelujah" went up.

The catch of the day rested safely in a wooden box with holes bored in it. This box, sunk in the river and secured by a rope tied to the bow, kept the fish William and I caught alive and fresh.

That night, after a supper of fried trout and perch, the men rolled up in their blankets, turned their feet toward the fire, and were soon snoring.

I took a position as lookout where the sandy beach met the woods. Corporal García's death had left us shorthanded. All afternoon I had stayed busy to avoid thinking about Calderón's questions. Now, with nothing to do but scan the forest and think, my conversation with Calderón hounded me.

I would soon meet my grandfather, the man who had held a grudge against my father for fifteen years. I shivered at the thought.

Chapter Fifteen

Two weeks later, I dangled my legs over the flatboat roof and read a book for young military surgeons about camp hospitals.

On the deck below, Calderón, his arm in a sling, chatted with a Spanish corporal. Day by day, Calderón grew stronger, as did William. Full recuperation would take at least three months. Luckily, gangrene had not set in. I seriously doubted I could saw off a man's arm or leg if I had to.

The farther north we traveled, the colder it became. Every morning, a heavy frost dusted the ground.

A distant boom echoed across the water. Clouds of geese and ducks exploded skyward from an island a half mile upriver. Expecting to see signs of a gathering storm, I scanned the sky. Nothing. Not a single cloud.

Within seconds, another boom thundered, closer this time.

Calderón whooped like an Indian.

The man has gone mad, I thought as I watched him scramble around the boat.

"Return the salute!" he ordered.

Two Spanish soldiers dutifully fired the cannon over the port bow.

Calderón grinned up at me. "Look! Fort Arkansas."

A half-mile away, barely visible in the morning mist rising off the river, a fort high on a hill loomed into view.

I suddenly understood Calderón's excitement. Fort Arkansas served as halfway point between New Orleans and Spanish Illinois. For us, it was no more than an overnight stopping point to get fresh supplies, but for the first time in weeks we would see fresh faces. The idea of sleeping inside a fort instead of on shore under an armed guard thrilled me.

The fort was made of upright logs chiseled to a point at the top, no doubt to discourage Indians from scaling the walls. Four guard towers, two stories tall, cut with small square windows, stood at each corner. Spain's castles and lions flew from the flagpole in the center of the parade ground.

By the time we pulled the flatboats to shore, Spanish soldiers had rushed out the front gate to greet us, their faces beaming.

Equally glad to see them, we hopped onto dry land.

The Spanish captain, the highest-ranking officer present, threw military etiquette to the wind. "Welcome to Fort Arkansas! We saw you round the bend. We've been expecting you." His voice shook with excitement. He locked Calderón in a Spanish-style embrace, despite his wound. They hugged and pounded each other's backs.

Calderón introduced me and William to Captain Cruz.

"It is a pleasure to meet you," the captain said in impeccable English as he shook William's hand. He wrapped his arm around Calderón's shoulder. "This gentleman and I served together as pages at the Royal Palace when we were boys."

"What news have you of the Ohio River?" William asked.

"Scouts report winter has already set in. The Ohio has frozen over. It is icebound from the Falls of the Ohio north."

William's face sagged while several of the men grumbled.

"You will have to stay here until spring!" Captain Cruz exclaimed. "You will be our guests for the entire winter." His light blue eyes glowed with delight.

Forced to accept Cruz's hospitality, William ordered the men to unload the flatboats and store the cargo inside the fort.

Weary and disheartened, we trudged uphill through mud so deep that it nearly pulled the moccasins from our feet. Back and forth, back and forth through the fort's heavy wooden door we went. It took more than an hour to empty the boat.

Captain Cruz directed us toward our new home, the largest cabin on the post. Along the way we passed a pregnant Choctaw woman watching us from her cabin door. Apparently one of the soldiers had taken an Indian wife. Judging by the size of her swollen belly, I estimated the baby was due in about two months.

I looked all around me. One captain, six soldiers, and an Indian in the family way. This was the entire post.

Chapter Sixteen

Wrapped in a buffalo robe, I huddled near the fire to shake off a winter cold. A checkerboard separated me and Calderón. I looked up at William, who stood by the fire, warming his hands.

"What did you say?"

"I said I'm sending a letter to Colonel De Gálvez to let him know our progress."

"Or lack thereof," Calderón muttered.

It was November 30, and we had been at the fort for nearly a month. Unfortunately, it didn't look like we would leave any time soon. This was a soldier's life. Wait. Wait. Wait.

"How are you getting a letter to New Orleans?" I asked.

"By courier. Every two weeks, a soldier delivers messages to the garrison in New Orleans. He's leaving in an hour."

An hour. An hour to decide whether or not to write Eugenie. I remembered her goodbye kiss, but could I put any stock in it? Maybe she kissed me because she thought she'd never see me again.

I pulled my buffalo robe tighter, but it did little to block the freezing wind that whistled through chinks in the wall. It looked like the winter of 1776 would be a harsh one.

Calderón drummed his fingers on the checkerboard. "Are you going to move before the century is over?"

"Do either of you know what *'mon petit chou'* means?" I asked.

"It means 'my little cabbage,'" William said.

"Oh." Eugenie had called me a cabbage. And I thought she liked me!

William gave me a playful punch on the upper arm. "Lucky dog. 'My little cabbage' is a term of endearment. The next time a girl calls you *'mon petit chou,'* say *'Je t'aime, ma belle.'*"

"What does that mean?"

"Trust me. Those are words she will want to hear. If there's someone in New Orleans you want to write," William said, struggling to hold back a laugh, "you best get to writing."

Calderón threw his hands up in despair when I forfeited the game and hurried away in search of paper, quill, and ink.

November 30, 1776, Fort Arkansas

Dear Eugenie:

We have stopped at an outpost in Spanish Louisiana halfway between New Orleans and the mouth of the Ohio River. The soldiers' mission here is to cultivate the friendship of the Indians so they won't trade with the English.

You wouldn't believe how much game is in the woods. Venison. Buffalo. Elk. A man could live in the wild forever and never go hungry. The men go hunting every day and kill enough meat to keep the fort well fed. In my spare time, I teach Lt. Calderón English. In return, he teaches me French.

I miss you. Je t'aime, ma belle.

Lorenzo

November gave way to December. I thought a soldier's life glamorous until I spent the winter at Fort Arkansas. We grew so bored, we would bet on anything. We put a glass of water on someone's head and counted how many steps he could take without spilling it. We bet on how many days the courier would be gone. We even bet on which kind of bird would next land on the parade ground.

As a medic, I did little more than give out laxatives and liniments, clean and dress sores, and drain abscesses. Considering the way my stomach knotted when I treated patients, I seriously doubted medicine was my calling in life. And, frankly, the prospect that Cornflower would go into labor before we left scared me. I knew nothing about childbirth and had no desire to learn. Papá and I must have set a hundred broken bones, tended as many gunshot wounds, and doctored more ailments than I can recall, but we never once delivered a baby. When a soldier's wife had childbirth pangs, the married women who lived at the fort helped deliver the baby.

Unfortunately, Cornflower was the only woman at Fort Arkansas.

Every morning I made it a point to be on the parade ground where the garrison formed up. The bugler blew assembly, and soldiers gathered around the Spanish flag that snapped in the breeze. The sergeant called roll. At his barked order, the manual of arms began.

Excitement surged through me. I admired the military precision with which they drilled and envied them their blue jackets and white breeches. Despite the mundaneness of military life in wintertime, I longed to be a soldier.

When I turned around to head for breakfast, I found William and Calderón standing behind me, quietly watching me.

Just as we finished breakfast, William challenged me to a tomahawk-throwing contest.

"I knew you gentlemen were bored," Calderón said, downing one last sip of coffee, "but I didn't know you'd resort to such measures."

Moments later, we stood on the shooting range behind the barracks. Both William and I clutched tomahawks.

"Dead center in the cross beam," I said, calling out my

target. I took aim, stepped back, and hurled the weapon at a wooden barricade peppered with bullet holes.

Thwack! The tomahawk quivered to a stop in the place I'd indicated.

Calderón's lower lip dropped in amazement.

I sauntered forward and pulled it out. "Beat that, William."

"For the right amount of money," he replied.

"A Spanish pillar dollar," I suggested and stepped out of the way.

"You're on." William took quick, casual aim and threw. The tomahawk embedded itself in the slash my tomahawk had made. William burst out laughing. "Looks like the winter I spent with the Indians wasn't wasted."

I peered at the target. "I can beat you in a shooting match."

"Oh, yeah?"

At that, William and I brought out our muskets.

Calderón strode toward the barricade and pinned a three-inch square of paper to a plank in the center of the barricade. "Your target, gentlemen."

I measured my powder and poured it into the priming pan and down the barrel. I took the ramrod from its groove under the gun barrel and rammed a bullet to the bottom. With the ramrod back in place, I threw the stock to my shoulder.

Calderón watched me with keen interest. He lifted his brows and shot William a significant look.

"I have a Spanish pillar dollar burning a hole in my pocket," William said. "It tells me you will miss."

"I have a dollar that says I won't." I took slow, deliberate aim.

Flint struck the pan, igniting the gunpowder. A second later . . . crack! The bullet hit the paper dead center.

William whistled between his teeth and glanced at Calderón.

I examined the gold coin William flipped in my direction and slipped it into my pocket.

"Good shooting," William said, scratching his blond hair.

"It's no harder than hitting a squirrel in a tree," I said.

"'Course, that sure took long enough. Out in the woods, do you say 'Hold it there, Mr. Bear. Don't you move while I draw a bead on you, if you please. This may take a few minutes!'"

"You didn't say you wanted speed *and* accuracy. That's different." I was already reloading.

At the bark of my musket, men had come at a run from all directions. Spanish soldiers and Lambs gathered around us.

William cocked a brow. "Gibson's Lambs can fire three shots a minute and hit dead center each time."

"I can, too."

"Three shots a minute?"

"For the right amount of money."

"A dollar for every shot you fire in a minute."

"Double that amount each time I hit what's left of the paper."

William agreed.

I knew something he did not. A musketeer in the King's Rifles taught me to shoot when I was so small I had to steady the musket on a tree stump.

Calderón pulled out his pocket watch and snapped it open. "Three shots in one minute, starting . . . now!"

Knowing every eye was fixed upon me, I concentrated on the target and put their watchful eyes out of my mind. I fired, reloaded, fired, reloaded, and fired a third time, all in the allotted time.

William stared at the target in disbelief.

A shout went up from the Lambs.

"Congratulations," Calderón said in an amazed voice. His eyes held newfound respect. "I didn't know you could shoot like that."

"How do you think I made it all the way across Texas? By sheer luck?"

"No. I believe God looks after fools." A grin spread across his face, lessening the insult considerably. Calderón had a strange sense of humor.

"Well, gentlemen," William said, laughing. "I've learned my lesson. No more gambling with Lorenzo. He'll eat you alive, just like a gator." He fished into his pocket, extracted six Spanish pillar dollars, and poured them into my upturned palm.

I found their chink quite satisfying, but the murmured admiration of the Lambs was even more satisfying.

Chapter Seventeen

Two days before Christmas, the courier returned from New Orleans. He stood by the flagpole and called out the names of those lucky enough to have received mail. He called my name twice.

Holding my breath, I accepted the letters. One was from Colonel De Gálvez. The other from Eugenie.

Colonel De Gálvez's could wait.

December 13, 1776, New Orleans

Dearest Lorenzo:

What joy to receive your letter. I hope mine finds you well. I miss you and your sweet smile. I wish you were here.

Gibson is on his way home. Colonel De Gálvez released him two weeks after you left and put him on an American trading vessel bound for Philadelphia.

The ship brought news of the war, all of it bad. The British landed in New York City and nearly captured General Washington. A twenty-one-year-old schoolmaster named Nathan Hale, a spy for the general, was hanged by the British. His last words were "I only regret that I have but one life to lose for my country."

Governor Unzaga will soon retire. He wants Colonel De Gálvez to take over his position as governor of Louisiana. The salary is generous and will give Colonel De Gálvez enough money to start a family. He has written to King Carlos for permission to marry the Widow De Saint Maxent. It is the perfect match. News has seeped out somehow, and the people of New Orleans are delighted. They have always loved Colonel De Gálvez because he speaks French fluently. Taking a French wife only endears him to them more.

Take care, Lorenzo. I am proud that you serve the Americans' cause of liberty. Write me soon.

With all my love,
Eugenie

I savored Eugenie's last words. She loved me. She worried about me. She was proud of me.

As I sharpened a quill with a penknife, I looked around for something interesting to write about.

The Lambs were engaged in various activities. One man changed the flint on his musket while another mended his greatcoat. In civilian life, these men were blacksmiths, farmers, coopers, tailors, tavernkeepers, and millers who had never traveled more than twenty miles from their homes.

I recalled Benjamin Franklin's words when he signed the Declaration of Independence. *We must all hang together, or assuredly we shall hang separately.*

From the British point of view, anyone who helped the American rebels was a traitor. Like Nathan Hale, I would hang with them if captured.

Chapter Eighteen

Christmas Eve, 1776
Fort Arkansas

My dearest Eugenie,

Happy Christmas. How I wish I were in New Orleans with you.

We are all well here and anxious to be on our way. Once a week a scout goes upriver to see if the Ohio is passable yet. As soon as

I had barely put pen to paper when Private Valdés, Cornflower's husband, bolted into the room. Wild-eyed with desperation, he headed straight toward me, seized me by the upper arms, and pulled me from my chair.

"She's having pains. The baby!"

My worst nightmare was coming true. Treating the Lambs for various and sundry ailments was one thing. Bringing a new life into the world was another. I stared at him in sheer terror.

Calderón eyed me curiously, as if he knew I was less than enthusiastic about my impending medical duties.

With a casual air, although my heart beat furiously, I retrieved Papá's medical bag from the room Calderón and I shared and followed Cornflower's husband to a one-room cabin along the fort's south wall.

Calderón, with nothing better to do, trailed behind me like a pup following its master.

Just as we entered, Cornflower let out a shriek and grabbed hold of the mantel with one hand and her belly with the other. Private Valdés froze in place. Calderón retreated one step. By the look on his face, he regretted tagging along and was about to bolt.

When Private Valdés came out of his daze, he rushed to her and touched his fingertips to her sweat-soaked cheek. For almost a minute, she stood there, mashing her lips together, her face twisted in pain. Then she relaxed and exhaled deeply. Solemn-faced, she greeted me in Choctaw.

I returned the greeting. Remembering Papá's routine when we visited patients, I went to the tin basin, rolled up my sleeves, and scrubbed my hands with lye soap and water. The rough, strong-smelling soap made my skin tingle.

Calderón followed my lead and dried his hands on a towel. He looked back at Private Valdés and Cornflower. "Do you want me to leave when you examine her?" he whispered in my ear.

"Examine her?" I squeaked. That was the last thing I wanted to do. "No. I might need your assistance." And besides, I craved Calderón's moral support.

"Have you ever delivered a baby before?" he asked, suddenly suspicious.

I leaned close to Calderón so my patient wouldn't hear. "Not exactly."

"Not exactly?" he repeated in dismay.

"I once saw a calf being born," I admitted. "How different can this be?"

Calderón opened his mouth, but shut it again, apparently not knowing how to answer that.

"Do you know how to do this?" I asked hopefully.

"One of the ladies-in-waiting at the Royal Palace went into labor while I was on duty. I think they timed her contractions."

A feeling of impending doom settled over me. We were two blind men stumbling in the dark.

I strolled over to my patient and smiled. "When did the pain begin?"

"An hour ago."

Nodding, I took her wrist to take her pulse. From previous conversations with her, I knew her first two babies were born dead.

My little stillborn brother flashed into mind. At the time, I was too young to remember what he looked like or to recall his funeral. All Papá ever said was that he came three months premature and never had a chance at life. I had only vague recollections of my mother dying a little later from complications.

Please God, please God, please God! I inwardly chanted. *Let the baby be all right. No complications.*

Cornflower's husband stood off to the side, wringing his hands, absolutely useless. Color drained from his face. He swayed like a sapling before a strong wind. A nervous father-to-be about to faint was the last thing I wanted on my hands, and, besides, I was nervous enough for both of us.

A contraction made Cornflower cry out in pain.

Her husband turned even whiter. Now I understood why fathers were never allowed at the delivery. Pacing back and forth in the hall where they could do no harm was their proper place.

An old memory came to mind. Papá once told me of a midwife who used ground-up rattlesnake's rattle to ease childbirth pains. Maybe it worked and maybe it didn't. At this point, I'd try just about anything.

"Valdés, I need a rattlesnake's rattle. Ask around and see if anyone has one."

He stood rooted for a moment, as if unsure he'd heard correctly, then dashed out. It was a fool's errand, but at least it would keep him occupied and out of the way.

Calderón cast me a questioning look. "What do you need that for?"

"Mostly it gets him out of my hair."

Calderón grinned and shook his head.

In preparation for this day, I had searched my medical books for information about childbirth. Dr. Jones's text only dealt with wounds and soldiers' ailments. *Gerald's Herbal* proved equally useless. I'd found the treatment for snake bite, the removal of warts, the cure for sunburn, but not a word about babies. Apparently, delivering babies was considered "woman's work."

With Calderón's help, Cornflower eased onto the woven mat that served as her bed. The language barrier did not seem to matter. Somehow they communicated. He sat beside her, wiped her forehead with a cool cloth, and spoke words of consolation in Spanish. She answered in Choctaw.

I understood them both. Since our arrival at Fort Arkansas seven weeks ago, I had absorbed a lot of Choctaw from Cornflower, the fort's cook, and the laundress.

The contractions came closer and closer together.

"How long for the baby to come?" she asked, the trust in me glowing on her face.

My courage returned. "Any time now." Feeling a blush grow, I did the one thing I'd dreaded the most. I took a fortifying breath and lifted Cornflower's skirt. I had avoided examining her private parts as long as I could.

To take my mind off what I was doing, I recalled the story Captain Cruz told me of Private Valdés and Cornflower's secret courtship. The lovers had eloped three years earlier, soon after they had met, and had taken refuge in the fort. Her father was somewhat less than pleased. At first, Captain Cruz feared the Choctaws would attack and take Cornflower back. He relaxed when her father, the chief, sent a brave to the fort with a message. The chief disowned her, said she had disgraced herself and her tribe, and could never return.

What a depressing story, I thought. And so many of its elements reminded me of what little I knew about my parents' courtship. I hoped the chief, unlike my grandfather, would put the past behind him once he had a grandchild and not hold a grudge.

My examination finished, I gave Cornflower a big smile. "It looks like we're going to have a baby soon." I sounded much more confident than I felt.

Her body grew rigid again, then went limp. A low groan of pain escaped her lips. Her hand tightened around Calderón's. He said nothing, although Cornflower squeezed so tight, his fingers blanched.

I felt my eyes bulge as I watched the baby emerge.

Cornflower was amazing. No yelling. No cursing. If I had been her, I'd have been screaming my head off.

Suddenly, a tiny, grayish baby girl with a mass of black hair squirmed in my hands, her wails puncturing the sudden quiet. With scissors from Papá's medical bag, I snipped the umbilical cord and tied it off.

Everyone talks about how pretty babies are. They must not have been talking about newborns. I thought she looked like a skinned squirrel.

After a close examination to make sure she was breathing properly, I handed her to Calderón and gave him instructions to clean her in the wash basin while I tended to the new mother.

He blinked down at the baby, talked to her in a hushed tone, and plodded away. After swaddling her in a cotton blanket, he laid her in her mother's arms. From that point on, Calderón and I weren't much use, except to clean up the mess.

Then came my second shock of the day. I never realized how much blood childbirth produced. It soaked my arms, the woven mat, everything within a three-foot radius. If I had been a woman, then and there I would have vowed never to have a baby. My stomach churned as I cleaned. Having done all we could, I slumped against the wall.

Throughout it all, Calderón showed a presence of mind I didn't think him capable of. He didn't seem to mind the gore.

At that instant, Cornflower's husband burst into the room waving a rattlesnake rattle. "Here it is!" He stopped. His eyes grew as large as Spanish doubloons. Ignoring me and Calderón, he hurried to his wife.

"Well, this certainly broke the monotony," Calderón remarked as he helped me repack my father's medical bag. "At least now you have something interesting to write Eugenie."

We said goodbye to the newly enlarged Valdés family and stepped into the inky night. Fresh snow blanketed the parade ground.

"I've never seen anything like that in my life." Calderón's voice quivered with excitement. "The way you handled yourself back there . . . I envy you. What a fascinating career you'll have."

I walked with my head bowed. Part of me was proud of my role in helping a new life into the world. Another part of me was more convinced than ever that I wasn't cut out to be a doctor. Several times I had nearly thrown up. I could still taste bile in my throat.

On and on Calderón prattled as we crossed the parade ground until I could bear it no more.

"It was an easy birth. All right? I didn't do anything spectacular. If there had been complications . . ."

"But there weren't any."

"But there could have been."

A chill wind rippled across the parade ground.

Calderón pushed open the door to our quarters. "You delivered that baby like you'd been doing it all your life." He stoked the dying embers and stretched his hands toward the warmth. "Maybe I should start calling you 'Doc.'" He glanced over his shoulder and grinned at me. "What do you have to do to attend medical school?"

I turned my back on him to avoid the subject. His question dredged up an uncomfortable memory. Papá always hoped I'd come to my senses, abandon my plans to become a soldier, and attend medical school in Scotland.

"Why does everyone assume I want to be a physician?" I said in a less-than-gracious tone.

Calderón seized me by the elbow and forced me around. "What is wrong with you? I asked a simple question and I expect an answer."

"I don't want to go to medical school, so just drop it," I warned, pulling away from him.

"You don't?" Calderón's voice conveyed surprise and disappointment. "Why not?"

"Because it's pointless. My father was a physician, but that didn't keep him from dying of consumption. He was a slow, deliberate man who never rushed a diagnosis or took chances with his patients. But he lost the two most important patients in the world. My mother and my little brother died in childbirth."

"I'm sorry. I didn't know that." Calderón gave my shoulder a little squeeze. "A physician can't save everyone. Life is full of risks. You have to be satisfied with the ones you *can* save."

For a moment, neither of us said anything. Then Calderón asked, "If you don't become a physician, what will you do?"

"I want to be a soldier."

"By all the saints! Why?"

"Because . . . just because!" In my heart, I knew why, but I could not put it in words. It had to do with duty, honor, freedom from foreign tyranny.

"Well," Calderón began in a conciliatory tone, "you could become an army doctor."

"And spend my life amputating limbs and digging out bullets?"

"And saving lives. See here, Lorenzo. You get to

choose between two careers. I envy you. If I could have chosen a career, it wouldn't have been the military."

I stared at him in disbelief. Calderón, the perfect officer in his ever-pristine uniform, the natural leader respected by all, didn't want to be a soldier?

He picked up a poker and jabbed at the fire, his eyes locked on the flames. "Last Christmas I was a page in the palace. I had good food, wonderful companionship, a comfortable place to sleep. Then, the next thing I knew, the king put me on a ship bound for New Orleans. In a heartbeat I went from the Royal Palace to this." Calderón waved his hand in a dramatic gesture, indicating our perpetually cold, dirt-floored cabin.

Thunderstruck, I turned toward him. "Did you do something to offend the king?"

"Quite the contrary. He has always taken an extraordinary interest in my future. The king believed I had a God-given talent for the army and gave me a commission. But I'm not so sure . . ." Calderón's face grew plum-colored. His gaze fastened on the toes of his boots. "Recently, I've been watching what you do and thinking . . . well . . . that medicine might be an interesting field."

So that was it. In a flash, I realized what a self-centered dolt I'd been. Calderón's question about medical school had been for himself, not me.

"To answer your earlier question," I said, "before you attend medical school, you become a doctor's assistant and learn all you can. You live in the doctor's home and take care of his every need. You roll pills and mix powders, gather roots and herbs, prepare bandages. In your spare time, you read in the doctor's library and learn the theories of medicine. The real training comes by accompanying the doctor on visits to patients. There, you learn the symptoms of disease and treatment. Of course, you don't have to attend medical school to set up a practice. Just look at me. I have some forty-three patients and no diploma. An apprentice does pretty much what you did back there with Cornflower. Watch and learn and be ready to do the physician's bidding."

He continued to study the fire. "So . . . have you ever considered taking on an assistant?"

"Honestly?"

"Honestly."

"The thought never crossed my mind."

Calderón swiveled toward me, his look expectant.

"Do you know what you're getting into? As a physician, you're called to a patient's bedside at all hours of the day and night. You'll never get rich. Patients often paid Papá in chickens, piglets, or eggs."

"Well, at least I wouldn't go hungry."

One thing about Calderón: he always found a bright spot in every situation.

"Oh, what the devil," I said as I thrust out my hand to seal the deal. "You'll have plenty of time to change your mind."

Calderón broke into an embarrassed grin and shook my hand. "Thanks, Lorenzo."

"I'm not sure I've done you a favor."

"You have. This is my first Christmas away from home. You and Cornflower made it a memorable one. Some day, I'll tell my grandchildren about delivering an Indian baby. I might even mention you were present."

Saying that, he retired for the night, leaving me alone with my thoughts. Last Christmas, Papá and I had visited Mexico City for the holidays. On my first Christmas without Papá I had delivered a baby and acquired a medical apprentice. Where would I be next Christmas? In Virginia with my grandfather? Or in Scotland, studying medicine at the University of Edinburgh, my father's alma mater?

I found neither possibility particularly cheering.

Chapter Nineteen

"Close the door, Lorenzo," William said. He ran his hand over his face and indicated with his chin that Calderón and I were to sit across the table from him. "Gentlemen, we have a problem." He flexed his jaw and studied the latest message from New Orleans. "Colonel De Gálvez just learned the British ambassador has sent a party of men to stop us."

"That would explain the Indian attack," Calderón said, "and the Redcoats we saw."

"But that was three months ago," I pointed out. "Would they wait so long to attack again?"

"Yes," William said, "if they have good reason to wait. Maybe they're setting a trap upriver. Maybe they're waiting for us to leave Fort Arkansas to avoid an international incident. As long as we stay on the left bank of the Mississippi, we are in Spanish territory."

"Or maybe they're waiting for reinforcements," Calderón suggested glumly.

Complete silence settled over the room.

"There's a British fort on the Mississippi just before we reach the Ohio River," Calderón said. "If I were the British, I'd gather my forces and launch an attack as we pass by."

"So would I." William scratched his beardless chin. "I need to know what the British plan to do. Someone must scout ahead and report back about their troop strength."

"I'll do it," I said.

I didn't miss the look William and Calderón exchanged across the table. They clearly expected me to volunteer.

William's gaze fixed on me. "Do you know what you're getting into? You're a civilian with this expedition, under no obligation . . ."

"Maybe not, but I'm the only one who can do this. Neither of you two can slip through the forest undetected. Your yellow hair," I said to William, "will give you away." I turned to Calderón. "The same goes for your brown hair. I can pass for an Indian." To emphasize my point, I wound a wisp of straight black hair around my finger. "Besides, I'm running low on opium and other drugs I can't get from the woods. Only I know which drugs I need."

"How well do you speak Choctaw?" William asked.

"Well enough to slip in and out of the fort," I replied, glad Cornflower had taught me the basics of Choctaw.

The rest of the day, we worked out a plan. By mid-afternoon, I looked like a Choctaw brave in leggings, breechcloth, and moccasins. My black hair hung in two braids, Indian fashion. With a buffalo cape around my shoulders and a gunny sack hidden beneath it, I headed for the pier.

The Lambs and the Spanish soldiers at the fort trailed after me, having gotten wind something was afoot.

Red ran a hand through his waist-long auburn beard and spoke the question that must have been on everyone's tongue. "Where you going dressed like that?"

I forced a smile. "Upriver to do a little scouting."

"Alone?" he asked, his disapproval evident.

William answered for me. "Alone."

"But, sir," Red began, "someone should go with him to make sure . . ." He trailed off when William's nostrils flared and his cheeks reddened with anger.

In the unnerving silence that followed, the Lambs exchanged scowls and gave William nasty looks. Apparently, they wanted to protest their commanding officer's decision, but knew they couldn't.

With that, I climbed into a canoe and took paddle in hand while Red untied its rope.

William wore a distressful look while Calderón mumbled something. Probably a prayer.

At first, I paddled with sure, strong strokes, but two hours of fighting the current rubbed my palms raw. I developed a keen appreciation for the Lambs' hard work rowing us upstream.

On the way upriver, I had plenty of time to think. Maybe this wasn't such a good idea. But I had to get opium and other drugs, and for that, I had to enter the fort. When Colonel De Gálvez and Captain Gibson stocked the flatboats with medical supplies, they apparently hadn't counted on the delay at Fort Arkansas.

By my third hour of paddling, a fort flying the British flag loomed into view on the right bank. Soon, the biting smell of wood smoke rode the breeze. English voices floated toward me. The closer I got, the stronger the smells and sounds grew. I breathed in a pungent aroma. Tonight the British would dine on venison stew. Normally, my mouth would water at the smell. Today, fear stole my appetite.

The fort's double gates stood wide open, guarded by two bored-looking sentries.

It was late afternoon by the time I tied my canoe to a tree. I hid in the underbrush. In the deepening twilight, I observed the fort and the Redcoats' daily routine. The fort swarmed with activity. Soldiers fetched water from the river, chopped wood, groomed horses.

The original plan that Calderón, William and I had worked out was simple. Study the fort, find a weak spot, and scale the wall. Now I saw that was unnecessary.

For an hour, I watched Indians come and go through the fort's front gate. So many entered, I lost count of them all. It looked like a gathering of many tribes.

Shortly before dark, a bugle called, announcing that the gate would close for the night. Everyone outside the fort hurried inside. The time had come. A sudden dryness settled in my throat.

Entering the fort proved surprisingly easy. When a band of five Indians approached, I fell in behind them. The sentries seemed not to notice me. Even so, my pulse raced and my breathing quickened as I stepped inside the enemy fort.

Chapter Twenty

A shiver coursed through me when the double gate slammed shut and a heavy wooden crossbar thudded into place, locking me in for the night.

Two rings of Indians sat around a roaring fire on the dusty parade ground.

Trying to look inconspicuous, I joined them and sat cross-legged on the outside row, hunched over, my buffalo robe drawn tight across my shoulders. For a long while, I watched everything and counted the Redcoats as William had suggested. So far, I had seen one officer, one sergeant, two corporals, and six privates. Like any frontier fort, the compound consisted of barracks, officers' quarters, stables, kitchen, and a wooden building with a tin roof.

What size force did we face? How many men were out of sight in the barracks? Or in the kitchen at supper?

Several Indians filled their bowls from the cauldron where stew bubbled and seethed, then returned to the circle.

The air shimmered in the firelight. Flickering sparks spiraled into the darkening sky and lit a six-foot-tall Redcoat leaning against the barracks door.

My blood chilled the instant I saw the jagged wound on his cheek. Saber-Scar. Here. Not more than thirty feet away, watching the Indians. His gaze swept over them and landed briefly on me.

My skin grew clammy with sweat and fear. What if he recognized me?

His eyes moved away to the man on my right. Looking disgusted, Saber-Scar turned and disappeared inside the barracks.

I blew out a sigh of relief and resumed my study of the compound. The building roofed with protective tin must be the supply room where gunpowder and ammunition were stored. If I could slip in there undetected . . .

A hand clamped down on my shoulder and jerked me from my thoughts. I froze.

"Little brother," a deep voice said, "who sent you?"

I jumped up and turned. A kindly, wrinkled face smiled at me.

"I am here to represent Chief of the Three Forks." With practiced ease, I repeated the line Cornflower had taught me.

"A long and tiring journey. You must be hungry. Eat." He pointed toward the cauldron.

I picked up a bowl and helped myself to the stew. Before I finished ladling it, two British soldiers, one an officer, the other Saber-Scar, emerged from a wooden building and strode toward me.

For a second, my heart refused to beat. Should I make a dash for safety? Stay still and hope Saber-Scar wouldn't notice me? Casually stroll away?

Amazingly, they brushed past me, hardly glancing in my direction. To them, I was just one more Indian brave.

In spite of my wobbly knees, I managed to return to my seat.

The British officer stationed himself in front of the fire and laced his hands behind his back. "Greetings, my brothers. On behalf of His Britannic Majesty, King George the Third, I welcome you." He paused.

A short, squat Indian leaned toward an elderly chief and whispered a translation in his ear.

The chief replied in Choctaw, and his Indian interpreter put his speech in acceptable English.

The words reached me, but I only half-listened to the

standard greetings and exchange of gifts. I was too busy memorizing every detail to tell William later. I suddenly realized why they hadn't attacked us. There were forty-three of us and only a handful of British soldiers.

In a long ceremony that involved speech after speech, Indians and British exchanged tokens of friendship. The elderly chief stood unsteadily and leaned on a brave's arm to deliver an address thanking the British for their hospitality. "By dawn's first light," he ended by saying, "we will return to our village."

Upon hearing that, the British officer stamped his foot like a spoiled child, and my attention snapped back to the proceedings.

"We fight a common enemy," he snarled. "An enemy who steals your land. Even now, they move up the Father of Waters on big boats. Have you seen them?"

The Indians shook their heads.

My spine tingled with alarm. Colonel De Gálvez was right. The British had learned of our departure and were searching for us.

"Your British father, King George, wishes us to live in peace, but there will be no peace if supplies reach the Evil Ones who invade your land and hunt your game. He expects you to fight."

A muscle worked in the old chief's jaw when he heard the translation. "Many braves have died for you," the chief responded. "We will die no more."

"By the new moon," the British officer countered, "King George will bring many soldiers to capture the rebels. There will be much honor to share and a double bounty for each rebel scalp."

The old chief seemed to consider that. "When the moon is new, we will return."

The new moon. Of course. That made sense. Under a new moon, troops could use the darkness to move into position undetected. Had the British finally learned how easy it was to spot their scarlet coats in the woods?

The flatboat flotilla had to leave now. If we waited too long, British reinforcements would arrive before we rowed past this fort.

The peace pipe passed from man to man, each one in the inner circle taking a draw, holding it, then expelling a long, gray plume. I'd heard of smoking the peace pipe, but had never seen it. I watched, fascinated, and took a draw when it was my turn.

The ceremony over, each Indian rolled himself in his blanket and made himself comfortable as best he could. The parade ground, littered with multicolored blankets, looked like a living patchwork quilt.

For some time, I watched the spangled sky and waited for the deep, rhythmic breaths that told me everyone had fallen asleep. I eased up and crept toward the supply door, hoping to find it unlocked. It was. At my touch, the door creaked open an inch. I hurried inside and gently closed it behind me.

Footsteps approached, heavy-booted British footsteps, not an Indian's soft patter. I held my breath and waited for the soldiers to pass by. Unfortunately, they decided to pause at the storeroom door for a chat. I wished I could see what they were doing. Worried that they might come in, I scrunched down behind a big barrel.

"Can we trust these savages?" That was the British officer speaking.

"If they say they haven't seen flatboats, then no flatboats have passed by."

I recognized Saber-Scar's voice at once.

"Where are those damn rebels?"

"We'll find them easy enough, sir. A half-breed boy named Lorenzo Bannister disappeared from New Orleans the night Gibson's Lambs slipped away. It's a good bet he's with them."

"A half-breed, you say?"

"He was raised in New Spain. Looks like he was

fathered off a Mexican woman. He's only about five-foot-six, and the men with him are all over six feet tall. He's the darkest one of the lot and will stand out like a sparrow among cardinals."

Saber-Scar didn't seem to know about the Spanish soldiers with the flotilla. At least he hadn't mentioned them so far. But he planned to use me as the way to distinguish our flatboat from others going up the Mississippi. What if we were captured because of me? The thought sickened me.

"Catching the rebels is all good and well," Saber-Scar went on in a low, confidential tone. "It will do wonders for our military careers. But the real prize is Little Lord Lorenzo."

"How so?"

"His grandfather is Judge Armand Bannister."

"Judge Bannister of Virginia has a half-breed grandson working with the rebels?" the officer asked in an amazed voice. "I know Armand Bannister. I know him well. He has never said he had a grandson." He chuckled. "So Armand's son mixed his blood with a Mexican. And a woman with Indian blood to boot. I don't wonder that Armand kept *that* secret."

"Before I left New Orleans," Saber-Scar said, "I wrote Judge Bannister and told him I'd found his long-lost grandson living in New Orleans. He offered to pay me handsomely for him."

"Of course he did. Judge Bannister is the richest man in Albemarle County." The British officer uttered a terrible curse. "You've fallen into a gold mine. I want a piece of this. If you and I deliver his grandson, we could retire from military service and live like kings. At all cost, we must capture the boy."

Not a shred of light penetrated the storeroom. The air around me grew close and hot. Even so, a chill surged through me when I heard those words. After a moment, I heard Saber-Scar and the British officer walk away.

First things first, I told myself. As soon as I returned to Fort Arkansas, I'd tell William why we had to leave immediately. Right now, I had to concentrate on finding the medicine and getting back downriver.

Like a blind man, I felt my way around the room until I touched glass, cold and smooth. Afraid that a light would give me away, I resorted to pulling out the stoppers and taking a gentle whiff to determine the contents of the bottles. I tested vial after vial, rejecting some, slipping others into my gunny sack. As quiet as a rabbit, I headed toward the now-smoldering campfire to find a way out of the fort.

The sight of a sentry on patrol at the front gate stopped me short. On the second-story platform, a guard leaned over the east wall scanning the forest. His musket rested against the upright logs sharpened to a point. I wheeled around in the shadows and climbed a wooden ladder to an unguarded platform along the opposite wall. I leaned forward. Casting a quick eye over the ground below, I judged the drop to be seven feet or so. I saw nothing that resembled a soft landing spot. The jump wouldn't kill me, but I might twist an ankle or break a leg. I decided to look for a better way out. I turned around in time to see Saber-Scar saunter out of the barracks. He unbuttoned his pants to relieve himself on a post and looked up. Straight at me.

Our eyes made contact. He angled his head questioningly and started toward me. Steeling myself and clutching the gunny sack to my chest, I climbed between two sharp-pointed logs. Just before I dropped over the side, Saber-Scar shouted, "Guard!"

I landed with a bone-jarring thud, picked myself up, and trotted toward the forest. Worry and fear for my life spurred me on. I had to get back and warn William. We had to set out at once or we would be captured.

At the edge of the clearing, with the fort about fifty yards behind me and the safety of the woods a few yards away, I heard a loud pop and felt a burning sensation in my back.

I'd been shot.

Chapter Twenty-One

The bullet's impact pitched me forward, face down in the leaves carpeting the forest floor. Instinct urged me to get up, but pain as hot as a branding iron shot through me every time I moved.

Back at the fort, confusion reigned. Someone bellowed out, "Who fired that shot?" while another voice roared, "Bugler! Sound the alarm!"

I heard the muffled sound of feet running toward me. Someone knelt beside me and muttered curse after curse. He lifted me as if I were no heavier than a feather pillow and cradled me in his arms.

My head lolled back. Overhead I saw twining tree branches move at a dizzying speed. I was only vaguely aware he was taking me into the woods, in the direction of the river. And then I heard a second man, barely visible in the starlight, urging him on in broken English.

Every footfall brought a sharp stab of pain. I bit my lower lip rather than cry out. I could think of nothing, other than how much I hurt. I raised my head and for the first time realized who was carrying me.

"Red," I mumbled.

"Hold on, Mr. Bannister. We're almost there."

At the riverfront, he laid me on my stomach in a canoe.

The second man whispered in Spanish, "Lorenzo. It's me. Héctor. Héctor Calderón. Brace yourself. This is going to hurt." He packed leaves into my wound and pressed his hand to my back to stop the flow of blood.

A thrashing sound, no doubt pursuers coming through the woods, drew closer.

"Shove off," Calderón said to Red in a panic-filled voice.

Red obeyed without question.

Slap! Slap! Paddles struck water with the greatest urgency.

A bullet ripped through the canoe's side above the water line. One after another plopped into the water around us, sending up misty sprays.

I struggled to stay conscious so I could make Calderón understand the danger we were in. "British troops. The new moon. Must go now. Saber-Scar's here. Trap."

"By all the saints," Calderón whispered. "I understand. Just relax, Lorenzo."

Darkness covered me like a shroud.

⊰⊱ ⊰⊱ ⊰⊱

A cool rag gently wiped sweat from my forehead.

"Everyone! He comes to."

I winced at Calderón's loud, stilted English.

Bright sunlight streamed through an open window and hurt my eyes. With it came the beat of oars against water.

Disoriented, I scanned my surroundings. To my surprise, I found myself in the flatboat cabin, lying on my side in bed. Someone had wedged pillows around me to keep me from rolling over on my wound. The room's slow rocking motion suggested we were once again under way.

Several Lambs hovered over me, concern written in their expressions, while Calderón sat in a wooden chair by my head. In spite of their scraggly beards, unwashed faces, and uncombed hair, they had never looked so good. Even Calderón, who usually looked princely, hadn't bothered to shave.

Red squatted beside my bed, which put us at eye level. "How you feelin', Mr. Bannister?"

"Like I've been shot in the back."

Red glanced up at the other Lambs and grinned.

William leaned over me. "Red said you were running toward the forest when a big Redcoat on the ramparts saw you. Shot you with a pistol. Lucky it wasn't a musket. That would have done lots more damage. The Redcoat was hopping mad and cussing up a storm."

"Saber-Scar," I muttered.

"We dug out the bullet and saved it. Before you know it, you'll be good as new. This will leave you with a dandy scar."

"Thanks for sending Red and Calderón."

My rescuers shared a quick look and shifted nervously.

William shook his head, his mouth drawn tight in disgust. "I didn't send them. They followed you on their own and against my explicit orders. I should shoot them both for desertion and stealing military property. That canoe was not theirs to take."

"I'm glad they followed me."

Nothing in their expressions showed remorse for disobeying orders. To the contrary, they looked rather pleased with themselves.

"Well, yeah," William said with a slight smile. "They're lucky it worked out all right. But do you know what makes me maddest about the whole affair?" He continued on without giving me a chance to respond. "They went on this exciting adventure and didn't invite me along."

His remark broke the tension in the room. The Lambs grinned at each other.

William turned to the men crowding around my bed. "Don't you have something to do other than hanging around here?"

Man after man said goodbye and wished me a speedy recovery.

Red, the last one out, stuck his head back through the doorway. "I know I done wrong, not following orders, but I'd do it again if I had to, Mr. Bannister. Lambs look out for other Lambs."

William pointed toward the door. "Out."

I savored Red's parting remark. *Lambs look out for other Lambs.* He considered me one of them.

William turned back to me and shrugged. "Red's got a good heart, but a mind of his own. If we had military discipline like the British army . . ."

"The British know about us," I said, my voice taking on a sudden high-pitched tone.

He gave me a reassuring pat on the shoulder. "Yes, I know. We'll be well past the fort before British troops arrive to reinforce them." Giving me a gentle smile, he left me alone with Calderón.

"Well, you made quite a spectacle of yourself," Calderón remarked with an infuriating little smirk.

"What do you mean?"

"Don't you remember how you ranted on and on in the canoe about British plans to ambush us? When we returned to Fort Arkansas, you grabbed William's shirt front and shouted 'The British are coming! The British are coming!'"

A flush of embarrassment settled over me. "You're making this up as you go along!"

"I am not!" Calderón replied indignantly. "You were like Paul Revere without the horse. You should have heard yourself. After we patched you up and reloaded the flatboats, we set out." Calderón laced his hands behind his head and studied the ceiling. "If you don't remember that, you probably don't recall asking me to write a letter to Eugenie."

My embarrassment grew. I could only imagine the idiotic things I must have said. "No. What did I write to her?"

"Nothing. I composed the letter myself while the men attended to last-minute details. An epistolary masterpiece, if I say so myself. Brief and to the point."

"Did you tell her I was hurt?"

"Oh, yes. I had to explain why I was writing in your stead. Not to worry. I portrayed you as quite the hero. Don't forget to write your fiancée as soon as you reach Virginia. That's what I promised her in the letter."

"She isn't my fiancée."

He tilted his head and cocked a brow. "Oh? The way letters have been flying back and forth between you two, I assumed a wedding was in the offing."

I focused on the raccoon-skin haversack on the ledge next to my medical books. Inside were Papá's correspondence and the six letters I had received from Eugenie. She knew I planned to join the army when I turned sixteen. Would she like to be a soldier's wife? My employment as medic ended as soon as we reached Fort Pitt. I needed a steady income so I could support a wife and family.

To judge by Calderón's growing smile, he knew what I was thinking.

"Those French women are charmers who will steal your heart. Just ask Colonel De Gálvez. You and Eugenie have a lot in common. Both orphans, alone in the world, in need of companionship and a family. She isn't a blueblood, but then again, neither are you. It's the perfect match."

"When did you become Cupid?"

"Who do you think introduced Colonel De Gálvez to the Widow De Saint Maxent? Eugenie's a pretty girl. Looking at her across the breakfast table every morning wouldn't be a chore."

To turn the conversation to a less embarrassing topic,

I asked, "What became of the medicine I stole?"

"Only one bottle broke on the way here. The rest is over there, on the shelf. We used some of it to doctor you. Kind of funny, don't you think? You know, 'Physician, heal thyself.'"

"Very funny," I said in a sarcastic voice.

"Well, maybe it's not funny to you now, but someday you'll see the humor in it."

In an odd sort of way, I could appreciate the irony. When I went for that medicine, I never imagined I'd be the first patient to use it.

Chapter Twenty-Two

Weeks and weeks went by. We didn't see a soul, not even an Indian. Little by little, my wound healed. I exercised and worked hard to regain my strength. Even so, now and then I experienced a twinge of pain.

One spring day, William shaded his eyes with his hand and called me and Calderón to the front of the flatboat. "Look, gentlemen!" He pointed to a river a thousand yards wide flowing into the Mississippi. "There's La Belle Riviere. The beautiful river. That's what the French call it. The Indians call it the Ohio."

"What does Ohio mean?" I asked.

"River of blood."

"I pray the name isn't an omen," Calderón said.

Where the Mississippi and the Ohio rushed together, there were no hills or mountains, only flat and swampy country.

"Over there," William added, "is Kentucky. Its name means the 'dark and bloody ground.' Some of us plan to petition Governor Henry . . ."

"Patrick Henry?" I interrupted. "The one who said 'Give me liberty or give me death?'"

"One and the same. We want to make Kentucky a county of Virginia. They've promised us land when the war is over. I plan to head to Kentucky with George Rogers Clark and stake out a claim. Kentucky. That's the place to be. Ole King George says we can't move any farther west, but the east is getting too crowded. You can't set foot outside your cabin without running into someone." He nudged me in the ribs. "Only a thousand miles before we reach Fort Fincastle."

Calderón and I shared a look of dismay.

"No one said we would stop at Fort Fincastle!" I protested.

"We go to Fort Pitt," Calderón said in stilted English. "My orders say to unload at Fort Pitt."

"I'm sure they do," William replied in an amazingly calm tone. "But first, we must stop at Fort Fincastle to see if it's safe to go to Fort Pitt. If not, we unload at Fort Fincastle."

"God in heaven!" I exclaimed. "I have to get to Virginia."

"Fort Fincastle *is* in Virginia," William explained as he uncurled a map. "On the banks of the Wheeling River. It's Virginia's westernmost outpost on the Ohio." He pointed to a triangle of land further upstream in Pennsylvania where the Allegheny and Monongahela Rivers met. "And here is Fort Pitt. It's the depot for most of the provisions for the western armies. Me, Gibson, and our men are posted there."

"Where is General Washington?" I asked.

"There's no way to know for sure. Probably here." William tapped a spot on the map. It read "Valley Forge."

I looked up from the map with dismay. "If you don't know where he is, how are Calderón and I to find him?"

William gave me an indulgent smile. "An army on campaign leaves a trail a blind man could follow. You'll find him."

"If I can find him so easily, won't the British track him down, too?"

William laughed. "Washington is an old fox on his own territory. The British will never catch him."

I hoped he was right. I looked forward to handing the general the letter from Colonel De Gálvez, but the closer we came to Virginia, the more I came to dread meeting my grandfather.

And so we traveled on. Time crept by. We caught pike, sturgeon, eels, and soft-shelled turtles with seines, baskets, trotlines, and hooks. We shot geese and ducks and roasted them over the fire. It all tasted delicious, but I longed for the shrimp and oysters of New Orleans. And I missed Eugenie.

Then one day in early April, I detected a faint roar ahead of us. The closer we drew, the louder it became. At first, it sounded like a roomful of people, all talking at the same time. Then I realized we had reached the most dangerous part of the trip. The Falls of the Ohio lay just ahead.

Chapter Twenty-Three

Swirls of water tossed the flatboat about. A wet wind slashed my face, but I couldn't wrench my gaze from the falls a half-mile away.

Rapids stretched from shore to shore and resembled a huge, wet stone staircase. Their descent was gradual, with no drop more than twenty feet, over water-smoothed rocks. Had we been going downstream, we could have shot the rapids safely. Unfortunately, we were going up that stone staircase.

No matter how hard the oarsmen rowed, the river current propelled us backwards. We ran the risk of being sucked into a whirlpool. Should that happen, it would be impossible to break free from the water's tornado-like suction.

"Pull to shore!" Calderón yelled over and over. Unable to make himself heard over the water's roar, he went from man to man, shaking their shoulders to get their attention, then jabbing his finger at the riverbank.

As soon as we touched dry land, the great portage around the falls began. While Spanish soldiers stood guard against attack, on constant lookout for Redcoats, the men unloaded the boats. Grumbling and cursing, they pushed and pulled and dragged and carried supplies to the edge of the woods.

It took two days to fell trees and fashion them into makeshift wagons. Once our lading was piled into them, the men hauled with all their strength and weight to move everything around the falls. That took another two days.

All the while, Calderón paced the shore like a soul in purgatory. I think he sometimes dozed standing up, but in the main, fear of attack stole his sleep.

Since heavy work might break open my nearly healed wound, I stood guard with William.

Finally, it was all over. Cargo, flatboats, and men rested in a quiet cove where a creek emptied into the Ohio. I flopped down on a rocky ledge under a giant sycamore. William unslung his musket and joined me.

I gazed all around at flat, fertile land that gently descended to the river and offered an excellent harbor. I looked upstream and down, at trees lacy with new leaves, at an island thick with wild geese, at a ribbon of water shimmering in the sunlight. No wonder William thought this paradise.

"Two years ago," he began, "I came here with a group of surveyors from Virginia. We lived over there." He indicated an island in the middle of the river. "Set up temporary huts and built a stockade. When the war broke out, I felt duty-bound to fight for Virginia. Some day I plan to settle in this spot."

Overhead, cardinals flitted from branch to branch. Wind tugged at my buckskin jacket. The sky was darkening fast.

"If you had a mill here," I remarked, "you could make a fortune taking flour to New Orleans."

"That's what I intend to do: make a fortune." William reddened and lowered his gaze. "I've got a girl back in Virginia. Her father thinks I'm a ne'er-do-well, but I'm going to prove him wrong." He threw a rock into the river. "She's Virginia aristocracy from one of the best families in Albemarle County." He paused. "And I'm not."

Not knowing what to say, I picked at the bark peeling off a giant sycamore in great scabs. "My grandfather lives in Albemarle County," I said after a moment.

William looked straight ahead. "I know. Calderón told me."

"Do you know my grandfather?"

William studied the ground. "Judge Bannister and I don't move in the same social circles."

We had been on the flatboat trip for months and William hadn't mentioned this before?

"What's my grandfather like?"

William shrugged and avoided looking at me. He inched away to watch a deer dip its head in the water. Suddenly, he cocked his head.

A long brrrrrr sounded from a bush about two feet behind him. A rattlesnake was coiled and ready to strike.

"Whatever you do, William," I said in the calmest voice I could muster, "don't move. There's a rattler behind you."

I eased William's musket from the ground and put the butt snug against my shoulder. Carefully sighting along the barrel, I fixed the brass bead on the snake's triangular head and squeezed the trigger. The crack rang in my ear.

For several seconds, musket smoke obscured my view. Had I hit it? If I had missed and the snake had struck . . .

Calderón dashed over to me. "Why did you shoot? Did you see something?"

At last, the smoke cleared.

"Can I move now?" William asked over his shoulder.

"Yeah," I croaked.

William turned, unsheathed his long knife, squatted by the snake, and began to skin it. "Look at this, Lieutenant. Lorenzo saved my life."

Calderón took a cautious step forward.

"Blew its head clean off," William said. "Big feller, too. Must be five feet long." He looked up at me with a jolly grin. "Thanks, Lorenzo. I owe you. What do you want made of the skin? Belt? Hatband?"

I stood there for a moment gaping down at him without answering. Calderón and I exchanged a look of dismay. Didn't anything scare this man?

William sliced off the rattle and tossed it to me. "Here. Use this to impress the girls. Tell 'em how you saved my life."

I swallowed hard and stashed it in the rawhide pouch around my neck, next to the Spanish pillar dollars I'd won off William.

Chapter Twenty-Four

The last few days of the journey along the Ohio, the oarsmen, anxious to be home, rowed a little harder. William, on the other hand, grew uncharacteristically grumpy the closer we came to Pennsylvania. And civilization.

At eleven o'clock on the morning of May 2, 1777, I stood guard duty on the bow. I tensed when a dim figure on the right-hand shore came into view, but soon relaxed. It turned out to be an elderly black woman, barefoot, smoking a huge corncob pipe and fishing from the bank with a cane pole.

Our flatboat rounded the bend, and there sat Fort Fincastle on the banks of the Wheeling River. We had traveled over six hundred miles from the Falls of the Ohio.

Built of squared timbers, Fort Fincastle appeared about a quarter-acre in size. Round portholes evenly spaced along the top allowed soldiers to snipe at attackers. All around jutted tree stumps where the forest had been cleared to make room for the fort.

As we approached, we heard the sound of feet running from all directions. Through the double wood door of the log fort. From further up the riverbank. Out of the nearby woods. Stomping, shifting, anxious feet that could hardly wait for us to dock.

I blinked, unable to believe my eyes.

On the shore, in his usual buckskin, moccasins, and coonskin cap, stood Captain Gibson, his arms folded across his chest.

"What took you so long?" he yelled to William. "I could have walked it faster than this."

"Look, Captain," William began.

"Captain?" Gibson interrupted. "Curb your tongue, sir! It's now Major Gibson."

We stepped ashore amid grinning faces, a hail of questions, introductions, and congratulatory slaps on the back.

We had delivered much-needed gunpowder and medicine safely. It felt good to be heroes.

Gibson took William's hand and pumped it. "Congratulations, Captain Linn." He emphasized the word "captain."

William blinked at him a minute before he broke into a grin. "Captain? I've been promoted to captain?"

Playfully, Gibson slugged him on the upper arm.

"Captain William Linn," William muttered. "Captain William Linn," he repeated, as if he couldn't get used to the sound of it.

Gibson smiled down at me. "Good to see you again, Gator. You've grown."

"What are you doing here, sir?"

"Waiting for you. After the flatboats left, Colonel De Gálvez released me from jail. I took a ship with a thousand pounds of powder by sea to Philadelphia while you headed upriver with the remaining nine thousand pounds. One way or the other, supplies would reach General Washington. In Philadelphia, I learned the Ohio was frozen. Knowing you wouldn't arrive until spring, I took leave, visited my family, then came here to wait for you."

Leaving the Lambs to unload with the soldiers' help, William, Calderón, and I received Lieutenant Colonel Marlborough's welcome and praise for a job well done. He escorted us past barracks and into officer quarters.

The aroma of venison stew and fresh-baked bread wafted toward us. My mouth watered. I hadn't tasted fresh-baked bread since Fort Arkansas.

By the time we set foot in Lieutenant Colonel Marlborough's cabin, the old black woman I had seen by the riverbank was setting the table. She wore a floor-length calico dress and a bright red turban around her head.

I held pewter bowls while she ladled a delicious-smelling stew into them from a giant kettle hanging over the fire. I couldn't help but notice her skin was only slightly darker than mine.

"This is the best meal I've had in a long time!" I remarked.

Lieutenant Colonel Marlborough sat at the table and waited to be served. He pushed light blond hair from his ghostly pale face. "I'm blest to have Aunt Mary as my servant."

Servant? She was a slave, pure and simple. But no one used the word "slave" because it wasn't considered polite. No matter which word you used, she wasn't free.

Why was I free and she wasn't?

"Aunt Mary has been with me since I was a boy," Lieutenant Colonel Marlborough went on. "She's like one of the family."

I glanced at Aunt Mary. Her sad expression reminded me of the look I'd once seen on a badger caught in a trap.

How Papá hated slavery. I recalled him saying, "It isn't right for one person to own another." And another time, he told me about Cincinnatus. My grandfather bought him several years before Papá's birth. When Papá came back from medical school in Scotland, he wanted to buy Cincinnatus and give him his freedom papers, but my grandfather refused to sell. "Cincinnatus was like a second father to me," Papá had once told me.

Between mouthfuls of stew, Lieutenant Colonel Marlborough asked about our trip. We answered all his questions and supplied him with information for future flatboat flotillas.

In return, he shared the latest war news. Washington's ragged soldiers had soundly defeated the British at Trenton and Princeton on January 3, 1777. Our first victories had changed the course of the war. Once word traveled to the Continental Army that we had brought Spanish supplies upstream under the noses of the British, morale would shoot up even more.

"Scouts have spotted British soldiers in the woods on the north shore," Gibson said as he sopped up the last of his stew with a chunk of bread. "One of them," he said, looking straight at me, "is your old friend Saber-Scar."

I frowned. "I wouldn't call him a friend."

Gibson chewed thoughtfully. "He and his fellow Redcoats are waiting for the flatboats to pass by. For that reason, we will unload the supplies here and transport them to Fort Pitt later."

"In that case, tomorrow I send my soldiers back to New Orleans," Calderón put in. "Lorenzo and I head to General Washington's headquarters."

Without further ado, Gibson unrolled a map and used candlesticks to hold down its curling corners. His fingers traced our route to Philadelphia. "General Washington is here. Daily, he expects the British to land at Philadelphia."

The remark threw a pall over the room.

The next day at dawn, Calderón's soldiers shoved off and headed down the Ohio. It would take them three weeks to drift with the current to New Orleans. It had taken us eight months to row upstream.

I packed my saddlebags and collected a $200 chit from William for my services as surgeon. Calderón and I prepared to leave on two horses he had purchased from the lieutenant colonel.

Sadness welled inside me when I shook everyone's hand and said goodbye. I would probably never see Gibson's Lambs again. Until this instant, I hadn't realized how attached I had become to them. I waved, but didn't say another word because I was afraid I would cry if I did.

Chapter Twenty-Five

On May 9, 1777, Calderón and I rode on horseback through the thick Pennsylvania forest outside Philadelphia in search of General Washington's camp. I listened to a woodpecker's rat-a-tat, a squirrel's bark, a raven's shrill cry. But the most annoying sound of all was Calderón's deep-toned voice drilling me on etiquette.

"When we reach the general's camp," he said, "watch what I do and repeat it. Address General Washington as Your Excellency. Keep a full pace from him and make no suspicious moves, or his bodyguards will have your head on a platter. Don't sit in the general's presence. If he invites you to join him, keep your feet firm and even. Don't cross your legs. Don't . . ."

"May I breathe?"

"If you must, do so quietly and in a gentlemanly fashion. Don't spit, cough, sneeze, sigh, yawn, blow your nose, gnaw your nails, or scratch in his presence."

"God in heaven! What sort of clod do you think I am?"

"The same goes for belching and wiping your nose on your jacket sleeve," he droned on.

"My father was a gentleman," I snarled, reining in my horse. "He taught me manners."

Calderón drew in his horse and twisted toward me. "And I served as page in King Carlos's royal household," he snarled back, "so I know how important etiquette is to a man of General Washington's rank. Try to act like a gentleman, and whatever you do, don't embarrass me."

Hot with anger, I urged my horse on, leaving

Calderón behind.

By the time he caught up, we had reached a clearing with large, fenced fields filled with newly sprouted crops of wheat, rye, barley, oats, buckwheat, corn, and potatoes.

I wondered what General Washington would look like. Papá had talked about him. A colonel in the Virginia militia, the Continental Congress had chosen him to lead the British colonists in revolt against their king, George the Third. Washington owned a big plantation named Mount Vernon, Papá said, with two hundred slaves. I couldn't understand how a man could fight for freedom, but own another human being.

Calderón and I followed a dusty road wide enough for an ox cart. In the distance, a church steeple peeped over the treetops. Houses of stone or brick loomed into view. We spotted an inn sign swinging in the breeze and stopped to eat lunch. Food and lodging were easy to find now as wayside inns became more and more frequent.

Calderón and I ate in silence at a common table with other guests and kept our search for General Washington to ourselves. You couldn't look at a person and tell a rebel from a Tory.

Afterwards, Calderón and I mounted up and turned our horses east. Shortly, we began to see missing rails from fences stolen by soldiers for firewood, boot prints, hoof-churned mud, smoke from campfires, all telltale signs of an army.

Without warning, a heavyset, mustachioed soldier stepped out of the woods and grabbed our bridles. "Halt and be recognized," he demanded. He wore a three-cornered hat and the blue-and-buff uniform of the Continental Army. Behind him stood a young rebel holding his musket at the ready. The second man wore green trimmed in gray and a black felt hat. They hardly looked like they belonged to the same army. Then I remembered William saying each colony had outfitted its troops in different colors.

Calderón drew himself up to his full height and said, "I am Don Héctor Calderón of His Most . . ."

The young rebel cut him off. "Sounds like a Hessian to me."

"He's a Spaniard," I quickly jumped in, hoping my Virginia accent would put them at ease. The last thing I wanted was to be mistaken for the German mercenaries King George had hired to fight the rebels. "This gentleman is my escort. My name is Lorenzo Bannister, and I have business with His Excellency, General Washington."

Ten miles back, Calderón had insisted upon changing from his traveling clothes into a dress uniform in anticipation of finding the rebels. I still wore buckskin, a round felt hat, and moccasins, in the false belief we were days from Washington's camp. Now I wished I'd changed, too.

The first man peered at Calderón, spat on the ground, and shifted his gaze to me. "What are you? An Indian?"

My straight black hair and dark skin coupled with a Virginia accent seemed to confuse them. Before I could explain, a large-featured, dignified man rode up, accompanied by two mounted men. He sat very straight on a big white horse. His strong hands held the reins loosely. A cape draped his broad-shoulders and hid most of his uniform.

The two sentries snapped to attention.

"Is there a problem, Sergeant?"

"Strangers, General."

I couldn't help but stare. Could this be General Washington? A shiver of excitement ran through me.

Fierce determination shone from his strong, proud face, but his eyes betrayed a great weariness.

Calderón swept the hat from his head and bowed. "Colonel De Gálvez, the captain general of Louisiana, sent us."

At the name "De Gálvez," the general's eyes sparked.

"Your hat, Lorenzo," Calderón whispered.

I yanked it from my head and held it over my chest. "An honor to meet you, Your Excellency."

"Gentlemen, welcome," he said with a grave nod. "I've been expecting you."

"You have?" The words popped out before I knew what I was saying.

Calderón shifted uncomfortably in his saddle and glared in my direction. It looked like he wanted to muzzle me.

"Major Gibson is a dear friend," the general said, looking straight at me. "I have known him and his family for years. When he came back from New Orleans, he advised me that a young man would bring a letter from Colonel De Gálvez." General Washington turned his horse.

We understood we were to follow him to camp.

My insides quivered, but if Calderón was impressed to sit beside so great a man, he hid it well.

We stopped at a large tent, and the general swung down from his horse. Upon his approach, the sentry on guard lifted the flap so the general could go inside. At six feet or so, he had to stoop to enter.

In spite of my excitement, I had the presence of mind to unbuckle my saddlebag and slip out *Gerald's Herbal.* The action made Washington's bodyguards tense, until they saw I was armed with only a book.

Calderón and I went inside with two bodyguards on our heels. One positioned himself at the back of the tent, while the second man lit a lantern hanging from a peg. He stayed close to the general, as close as a shadow.

I marveled at the general's tent. It held a small mussed cot, several wooden chairs arranged in a semi-circle, a cluttered writing table, a large trunk. He obviously could be packed and ready to leave in a matter of moments. All in all, the scene reminded me of my room when I traveled with Papá. Medical emergencies often called us away.

General Washington sank into a chair and indicated with a wave of the hand that he wished us to join him.

"Your Excellency," Calderón began when we were seated, "we have the honor to present Colonel De Gálvez's letter."

Recognizing my cue, I drew the letter from *Gerald's Herbal*, where it had safely traveled from New Orleans to Virginia, and handed it to the general.

He looked amused by its hiding place. "Mrs. Washington frequently refers to *Gerald's Herbal*." He slid a finger under the seal and looked from me to Calderón questioningly. "I assume one of you gentlemen has the formula."

As if on cue, Calderón slipped a vial from his jacket pocket, removed the stopper, and poured a solution over the page. Ink magically appeared.

Careful not to let the solution soil his clothes, the general held the letter far from him and re-examined it. "I have no Spanish. I presume the colonel instructed one of you to translate."

"That would be me, Your Excellency." I took the letter General Washington passed to me and began to read it aloud. "'September 21, 1776. New Orleans. To His Excellency . . .'"

"Go to the meat of the matter, son."

I wanted to look at Calderón and say, "See! He's not as stiff as you think. He called me 'son.'" But I restrained myself and read on.

"My king and master, as a friend of the liberties of America, requests that you respect his desire for strict secrecy. He further wishes to become the greatest and most generous ally of the United States. To that end, he informs you that it has come to his attention that the British monarch is attempting to purchase mercenaries from the Russian czar."

"This is important information," General Washington said, straightening. "It confirms a suspicion someone recently shared with me. I shall inform the Continental Congress at once. What else does Colonel De Gálvez write?"

I continued to read. "If, as I suspect, my king intends to send further supplies and messages to you, we will have need of a courier. If this reaches you, then we have found a worthy young man to serve as courier . . .'" My voice trailed away and my eyes jerked up from the paper. I was glad I was sitting, for my knees had suddenly gone weak.

The general smiled. "Please continue."

I swallowed hard and did as ordered. "'. . . as courier between us. We may safely rely on his firmness and fidelity. He accompanied Captain Gibson's company in the capacity of medic. I am sure he may yet render us a more worthy service. He speaks both Spanish and English and is a man of sterling character." Inside, I swelled with pride to think the colonel considered me a man. "I ask Your Excellency to give Mr. Bannister every assistance, as he is on his way to Virginia to meet his grandfather, Judge Bannister of Albemarle County.'" I paused to take a breath and looked up.

Odd. Suddenly, the general was frowning at me.

"Armand Bannister is your grandfather?"

"Yes, Your Excellency."

His countenance darkened. "I know your grandfather. I know him well." It sounded like the general regretted that.

I explained about my father's death and his final wish that I deliver a letter to my grandfather, whom I had never met.

"I see," the general said, stroking his lower lip. His expression softened. "Read on."

"'I respectfully urge Your Excellency to offer Mr. Bannister a commission at the rank of captain. It is my honor to be your humble servant, Colonel Bernardo De Gálvez, Captain General of Louisiana.'"

"How old are you, Mr. Bannister?"

For a brief moment, I considered lying. No sooner had the idea entered my mind than I dismissed it. A man of honor did not lie.

"Fifteen," I said despondently. "I don't turn sixteen until July."

"Fifteen," he said with a sigh.

Calderón, silent for so long, spoke up. "Mr. Bannister has wisdom beyond his years. I suggest you offer him a commission right away. He is a sharpshooter and an excellent woodsman. He would make an excellent soldier as well."

High praise from Calderón. A rare commodity indeed. I stared at him in amazement.

One side of the general's mouth pulled up in amusement at Calderón's passionate defense. "Unfortunately, I cannot enlist anyone until age sixteen, even on Colonel De Gálvez's recommendation." The general swung his gaze from me to Calderón. "Or on your recommendation, either."

Calderón blushed and lowered his eyes, no doubt thinking he had spoken out of turn. A lieutenant, giving a general unsolicited advice.

"However," General Washington went on, "I do need an agent in New Orleans who speaks Spanish and English. The flatboat flotilla you served aboard will be the first of many that will send supplies upriver from our Spanish friends."

Excitement pumped through me at the thought of more flatboat trips.

The general gestured toward me. "I wish you to take a letter to Governor De Gálvez."

"*Governor* De Gálvez?" I asked.

Calderón and I exchanged looks of surprise. So Colonel De Gálvez had replaced Governor Unzaga. What a feather in his cap.

A smile grew on my face as I assumed my place at the writing table. I was happy for the man who treated me like his son.

"Use this ink," the general said, pushing a glass bottle toward me. He cleared his throat. "Please accept my sincere thanks for your efforts on our behalf. A fortnight ago, the supplies safely reached Fort Pitt just before it came under British attack. Without those supplies, the fort no doubt would have been lost."

"Your Excellency, forgive my interruption," I said. "Were any of my Lambs wounded in the attack?"

General Washington pivoted toward me. "*Your* Lambs?"

My ears burned with embarrassment, but the general merely gave me an indulgent smile.

"I understand the attachment that forms when men serve together. No men were killed in action." He resumed his dictation. "I send my sincere gratitude . . ."

General Washington continued on, and I continued to write. As the ink dried, it disappeared. It turned out that he wanted to buy food for the Continental Army from Colonel De Gálvez.

Once the letter was finished, I eased it into *Gerald's Herbal*.

"I would be honored if you gentlemen joined me for coffee."

"The honor would be ours, indeed, Your Excellency," Calderón said.

The bodyguard stationed at the back of the tent left without a word, as if he had heard a silent order. Moments later he returned with a fresh pot of brewed coffee and four clay mugs.

"I would serve you gentlemen tea," the general remarked with a smile, "but nowadays, it's unpatriotic."

We all laughed.

A few minutes later, over coffee, Calderón and I told him about our flatboat adventure.

I took a sip of coffee and regarded the general over the lip of my cup. Either he was immensely interested in

Calderón's narration of the Indian attack or he was struggling to decipher Calderón's English.

A sudden thought entered my head. What if Papá could see me now? It struck me that he would be proud that General Washington had selected his son as his personal envoy to the Spanish.

Chapter Twenty-Six

The day I'd dreaded for so long finally arrived. Today, May 21, 1777, I would meet my grandfather.

At dusk Calderón and I reached the edge of my grandfather's plantation. Newly planted fields of Virginia tobacco, the finest in the world, stretched out before us.

Slaves dripping sweat hoed a field in the failing light. To my left I spied a man with a back scarred like Red's. I reined in my horse and shivered.

"What is wrong with you?" Calderón demanded.

I didn't answer. I merely shrugged.

Calderón and I continued on, my soul burdened by the sight. Papá said slavery was the main reason he left Virginia. I knew it was the custom of the day, but seeing it with my own eyes, on my grandfather's land, sickened me.

A huge black man, bent beneath a load of wood, lumbered across the dirt road fifteen paces ahead of us. My gaze locked on an R branded on his cheek, then fell to his bare feet. Three toes on one foot had been whacked away. R must stand for runaway. The sight chilled me to the core.

Five minutes later, Calderón and I drew up in front of a three-story, gray stone building surrounded by lush flower gardens and neatly trimmed hedges. We dismounted.

Taking a deep, fortifying breath, I drew Papá's letter from my haversack.

An elderly house servant in blue-and-white livery descended the front steps, greeted us with a low bow, and attended to our horses.

"Good evening, my good man," I said. "I have a letter for Judge Bannister. May I speak to him?"

A tall, rawboned man rose from a rocking chair on the front porch. He stepped toward the white wooden railing and glared down at me. "What do you want?"

I knew who he was even before he identified himself. He looked so much like Papá. I hadn't expected that. The same fair complexion, straight blond hair, and gray-green eyes. I guessed him to be about seventy years old.

"Sir," I began in my most gracious tone, "I am here on a private matter. I'm Lorenzo."

My grandfather drew a huge breath, and his hand flew to his chest. He took a step back. All color drained from his face. "Lorenzo?" he whispered. "So you came, after all. Cincinnatus!" he yelled to the slave at the foot of the steps. "I am not to be disturbed."

I pivoted around. So Cincinnatus was alive. How I wanted to talk to him. No doubt he was filled to the brim with stories about my father. But I could do that later. For the moment, I had other business.

Calderón and I climbed the steps, he in his dress uniform, I in a suit of clothes I had bought in Philadelphia after we had left General Washington's camp.

When my grandfather and I were within arm's reach, we stood unmoving, staring at each other.

Calderón looked from my grandfather, to me, and back again. His gentle smile faded into a frown of confusion, as if he had expected us to fall into each other's arms and put on a grand display of emotion. The awkwardness of the moment stretched.

"Let's go inside," my grandfather suggested.

Calderón started toward the front door. My grandfather stepped in front of him, arms folded across his chest, his expression sharp. "Not you, boy. You stay outside."

"Excuse me, sir?" Calderón's face turned cardinal red.

"Lieutenant Calderón is an esteemed friend," I said as I watched a vein pulse on my grandfather's forehead.

Calderón had insisted upon accompanying me to Virginia, even though his orders from Colonel De Gálvez said only to see me to General Washington's camp. His feeble excuse was that he'd never been to Virginia and wanted to see it. I suspected he had a good reason to delay his return to military duty in New Orleans, but I couldn't imagine what that might be.

Calderón directed a fierce scowl at my grandfather, the kind of scowl he had given me when we first had met. "I am in Mr. Bannister's employ. He hired me as his bodyguard to escort him to Virginia."

"Ah," my grandfather said, as if Calderón's statement made everything clear.

Out of the corner of my eye, I studied Calderón. Never did I imagine him to be such an accomplished liar, and I wondered why he embroidered the truth.

"Come inside and I'll pay you," my grandfather said, unblocking the door.

"Mr. Bannister paid me already."

Another lie.

I stepped toward Calderón to give him a typical farewell hug. He took a quick step backwards. I didn't know what to do or say. Had I somehow angered him? Embarrassed him? I thought we were friends, and friends always said goodbye with a hug.

"Goodbye, Mr. Bannister," Calderón said, giving me a deep bow. "I am glad to serve you." He slipped back into Spanish. "Do not tell your grandfather what I am saying. Something is not right here. Keep your guard up."

"Yes," I replied in English for my grandfather's benefit. "I will gladly send your commander a letter commending your services."

"Thank you." Calderón turned toward my grandfather and gave him a grandiose bow. "Goodbye, sir. It has been a great pleasure to meet you."

After nine months with Calderón, I knew him well. I also knew when he wasn't being himself. Whatever game he was playing, he was playing to the hilt.

Another goodbye. It both saddened and worried me to watch him walk away.

As I followed my grandfather inside, I noticed he had a slight limp and a nodule on his ear, two signs of gout.

A giant staircase rose from the entry foyer to the second floor. Oil paintings of richly dressed people lined the walls. One portrait showed a highly decorated British naval officer, his full lips pursed like a pampered child. My gaze fixed on it.

"That is my father," my grandfather said. "He was an admiral in the Royal Navy. He died in battle during Queen Anne's reign, when I was two years old."

A moment of illumination struck me. That would mean my great-grandfather died at the beginning of the century, during the War of Spanish Succession. Had he died fighting the Spanish? Did that account for my grandfather's dislike of Spaniards?

In the library, I lowered myself into a chair facing a large desk. A portrait of the British monarch, King George, hung in a place of honor behind it.

My blood pumped a little faster. My grandfather was a Tory, a British sympathizer. Had General Washington known that? Was that why he scowled when I mentioned my grandfather's name?

Feeling ill at ease, I gazed about the room. How should I start a conversation? What did I call him? Grandfather? Judge Bannister? Sir?

Maps of the British Isles, Europe, and Virginia lined the walls. A round window overlooked the grounds and offered a view of a garden just coming into bloom. Sunset fell on the Blue Ridge Mountains, making a warm picture in the distance. But an icy air hung inside the room.

My grandfather laced his hands together in a prayerful stance and leaned toward me. "You are Jack's responsibility. Where is he?"

I swallowed hard. "Papá passed away nine months ago from consumption." I waited for a reaction. A tear. A look of surprise. Or regret. After a long pause, I said, "He wrote you, sir, from Saltillo, Mexico, when we started our journey to Virginia."

"He said nothing about being ill, only that he was coming back."

I handed him Papá's letter. "On his deathbed, he asked me to deliver this."

During the long silence that followed, he unsealed it, read it, and refolded it. He forced a smile. "Your father asks me to use my considerable influence to find you a position. I presume you read and write."

"Yes, sir."

"Your father refused to serve His Britannic Majesty." He spoke slowly, as if choosing his words with great deliberation. "You can continue the Bannister tradition of service to the crown. I have friends in the Royal Navy. All I have to do is contact a certain individual I know."

"No, sir," I said with a firm shake of the head. "I have other plans . . ."

"The Royal Navy enjoys great prestige. Bannisters have always been navy men. Except for your father." He blew out a huge sigh that suggested Papá had disappointed him greatly. "This is your opportunity to correct his egregious error."

"Sir, my father was a fine man who did what he thought best."

"Is that so?" My grandfather stared at me, long and cold.

"Yes. He was an excellent physician . . ."

"Who served as lapdog for the Spanish army and mingled with the scum of the earth."

A red rage surged through me. I jumped to my feet. "My father saved many lives. Some of the bravest men

I've ever known were Spanish soldiers."

I also was thinking of my Lambs. They were not scum, but uneducated and uncultured men who had put their lives at jeopardy for American freedom. I bit my tongue, angry that I had to let his remarks go unchallenged, but I couldn't respond without giving away important information to a Tory.

My grandfather waved his hands in a conciliatory gesture. "I don't mean to speak ill of the dead. Sit down. I only have your best interests at heart."

I eased back into my chair.

He drummed his index finger on the desk. "I know of a planter from Alexandria looking for a private secretary. I'm sure he would give you the position if I recommended you."

"Sir . . . I have a position." I thought fast. How much could I tell him without giving away too much? "In New Orleans I worked as a scribe for an import-export firm. I have a position there." And Eugenie. Thinking about her brought a smile to my face.

Fingering my father's letter, he nodded, as if deep in thought. He rose and walked to the portrait of King George, a hinged picture that hid a wall safe. He spun the tumblers, opened the safe, and placed my father's letter inside.

How I wanted that letter. My father's last letter. My grandfather meant to keep it. Maybe it had great sentimental value to him.

"Well, boy," my grandfather said, turning, "you may stay the night, as I do not wish to turn you out into the dark. Mind you, I expect you to be on your way by tomorrow."

"Yes, sir."

I was as anxious to leave as he was to be rid of me. How could this awful person have raised a kind and wonderful man like my father?

"Let's go see that your horse is properly bedded for the night, and then we'll share supper."

It was full dark by the time we stepped out the back door. Lantern in hand, my grandfather led me toward a small brick building where the lawn met the woods. "Let's stop here, shall we? I'll have Cook prepare you a good breakfast to start your trip right." He unlocked the door and gestured for me to enter first. "Go unhook a ham."

No sooner had I stepped inside than something heavy crashed down on my head.

The dirt floor rushed toward me, and darkness enveloped me.

Chapter Twenty-Seven

It could have been five minutes or several hours later when I came to. My head throbbed. I pushed up from the ground, cold and hard beneath me, and stood unsteadily. My head brushed against something dangling from the ceiling. The smell of cured meat filled the air.

My grandfather had locked me in the smokehouse!

Sweat dampened my forehead. When I reached into my jacket pocket for a handkerchief, I realized I was no longer in my new suit of clothes. I ran my hands over my shirt and pants and found myself in a scratchy linen shirt and cotton trousers, the kind of clothes slaves wore.

"Oh, no!" I groaned. The rawhide pouch that hung around my neck on a rawhide string was gone as well. My grandfather had taken that too. It contained two hundred dollars, my entire salary as medic. Calderón and I had visited the Continental Congress in Philadelphia on the way so I could cash in the chit William had given me.

Feeling my way around in the dark, I found the door. My excitement melted into disappointment to discover the absence of a door knob.

There was no way out.

Black despair filled me. The walls closed in. Then suddenly, a key turned in the lock.

"The boy's in here," my grandfather said.

I shaded my eyes from the lantern light and saw my grandfather enter with a British naval officer on his heels.

Two armed redcoats, one with a musket, the other

with a billy club, stationed themselves by the door, effectively blocking the only exit.

Oh, God. No. My grandfather was selling me to a press gang. To make matters worse, I recognized one of them.

Saber-Scar leered down at me, the same way he had on the street in New Orleans. He knew me at once. A look of deep satisfaction spread across his face.

I recalled Saber-Scar's promise the day we met. *I'll get you if it's the last thing I do.* And now he had.

"Head down," he ordered. He stiffened and gripped his musket a little tighter when I did not immediately obey. "Now!"

I had no choice but to lower my head.

The officer orbited me and looked me over from head to toe as if I were a horse at an auction. He squeezed my arm muscles.

"He's a good boy," my grandfather said. "As docile as a lamb."

"Hmmpf!" Saber-Scar exclaimed. "I knew him when I lived in New Orleans. He's a troublemaker. In and out of jail constantly for brawling."

I wanted to protest this lie, but was in no position to do so.

The British officer lifted my chin with his riding crop and peered at me. "We shall see. Take off your shirt."

I forced down the panic rising inside me. In one motion, I pulled my shirt over my head.

"His back is clean," my grandfather said in a relief-filled voice. "He's never been flogged. As I said, docile as a lamb. The boy's been living in New Spain. Speaks Spanish like a native. If the Spanish enter the war," my grandfather said, an anxious quiver in his tone, "he could prove useful."

The British officer grunted in agreement.

"If you had done your job," my grandfather said to Saber-Scar, "I could have avoided the embarrassment of having him show up on my doorstep. I'm not paying you a damned farthing. Just get him out of my sight."

The British officer gave me an evil smile. "I'll make good use of him. He should serve me well."

Involuntary servitude on board a British ship! Panic mixed with anger set in. If I tried to desert, I would be flogged. If they found General Washington's letter . . . God in heaven! What had my grandfather done with it? Had he given it to the British?

"Put your shirt back on," the British officer ordered.

Before I could do so, Saber-Scar said, "Wait."

I froze.

"Look at this, sir."

The British officer stroked the scar on my back with his riding crop. His lips curled at the edge. "Shot in the back. Running away, were you?"

Saber-Scar's sharp intake of breath told me he had made the connection. An evil smile grew. "It was you," he said with sudden understanding. "You were at the fort. You must have overheard our plans. That's how the flatboat flotilla was able to evade us at every turn. How droll! We've been after you for a long time." Saber-Scar laughed out loud. "Sir! It would appear we have captured a rebel spy."

My heart sank. I knew what happened to spies. They were hanged.

Chapter Twenty-Eight

We traveled for half an hour on horseback with the British officer in front and the two Redcoats close behind. Slowed by darkness, we picked our way down a narrow dirt road through a pine-scented forest.

Why had my grandfather done this? Why did he write Papá telling him to come home if he hadn't wanted us back? I searched for an answer, but found none.

A plan. I needed a plan. With two guns behind me, escape was out of the question.

In my mind's eye, I saw Eugenie, gorgeous in her green ball gown. A warming thought. Something to hold on to. She loved me. She expected me to return to New Orleans some day. I had to survive this.

Something whizzed through the air past my ear. Ahead of me, a tomahawk buried itself in the officer's head.

Indians!

I bent low over my horse's neck for protection and swiveled around in time to see Saber-Scar slump and fall from his horse. Another tomahawk had found its mark.

My mount skittered to the side. Fearing he would bolt and throw me, I gripped the reins tighter. My knees dug into the saddle as I tried desperately to stay on. "Easy now," I coaxed.

An instant later, a sharp crack rang out, and Saber-Scar's companion fell dead.

My horse reared and pawed the air. I toppled off and felt myself sailing backwards. My arms flailed the air. I hit the ground with a bone-jolting thud. All the breath rushed out of me. For a split second, I thought I was dead, but the pain exploding through me meant I still lived.

Footsteps whooshed in the dry leaves that carpeted the forest. I spotted a half-dozen figures in the shadows.

Get up! my mind screamed. *Get up!* A survival instinct gave me the energy to stand. Groaning with pain, I darted toward the woods edging the road, racing blindly toward the lush undergrowth. Footsteps sounded behind me. I glanced over my shoulder. Several huge Indians bolted from the moon-cast shadows. They shouted and waved their arms frantically overhead. My heart hammered so loudly, I couldn't hear what they shouted. I crashed into the underbrush, my hands stretched in front of me to fight the vines and branches flogging my face.

In a burst of speed, the biggest Indian broke away from the others. He came closer and closer, then grabbed a handful of my shirt. I struggled to get away, but tripped on a tree root and fell face down. The giant landed on top of me.

At any moment I expected to feel a hatchet at my scalp line ripping the skin from my skull.

"Stay still, Gator. It's me."

Gator? Only one person called me that.

"Major Gibson?" I whispered in dismay.

"Are you hurt, son?"

"Son? I thought I was a gator. Does that mean I've moved up in the animal kingdom? Or down?"

"If you still have a sense of humor," he said as he gently rolled me over, "you can't be too badly hurt." His hands deftly searched for broken bones.

"I'm not hurt at all," I bragged, although every muscle ached and I felt bruised all over.

Gibson helped me to my feet.

Moonlight shone on six faces painted with red berry juice. The "Indians" broke into a grin, relief etched on their faces.

I stared at Gibson, William Linn, Calderón, Red, and two other Lambs. Bare-chested, wearing breechcloths, leggings, and moccasins, they had smeared their hair with bear grease and streaked their faces with war paint. All in all, they made passable Indians.

Calderón wrapped me in a silent bear hug.

I couldn't tell for sure in the dark, but I think he was crying.

⊰⊱ ⊰⊱ ⊰⊱

"This one's alive," Red called out a minute later as he pulled the tomahawk from Saber-Scar.

Two Lambs dragged the corpses into the woods to let nature's predators dispose of their bodies.

Meanwhile, Gibson and William rounded up the Britons' horses and erased all evidence of the attack.

"Take him to camp," Gibson said. "He's valuable."

"My pleasure, sir," Red said.

Emotions tumbled through me as I watched them bind Saber-Scar's hands with rawhide and heft him onto a horse. Never before had I harbored so much hatred for a fellow human being. I wished him dead. But alive, Saber-Scar would buy the freedom of an American soldier held by the British. Dead, he was useless.

I watched Red and the Lambs ride away with Saber-Scar. "Thanks for rescuing me." I looked from William Linn to Gibson to Calderón. "How did you know I was in trouble?"

Calderón shrugged. "After the cold reception you received from Judge Bannister, it was obvious. General Washington told me to have my guard up."

"He did?"

"He feared you would be in great jeopardy," William said. "Armand Bannister is suspected of being a Tory."

I nodded. "He is."

"Red somehow got wind that you might be headed

for trouble." Gibson scowled at Calderón, suggesting a secret alliance between him and Red. "When he passed the word to the other Lambs, there was no way to stop them. It was either shoot them all for desertion or select a squad to rescue you."

I looked up at a bright moon inching across the sky. My chest constricted to think the Lambs had come to my aid.

Gibson touched my shoulder. "Let's get out of here. We need to get you on your way to New Orleans."

"No. I'm going back to my grandfather's house."

"What?" Gibson asked.

"He has my father's letter and my other possessions." I couldn't bear to think of my grandfather keeping Papá's medical bag and my raccoon-skin haversack that contained Papá's correspondence and Eugenie's letters. And I relished the idea of confronting my grandfather.

Calderón shook his head. "No. I won't permit this. It is too dangerous."

William shook his head, too. "No, Lorenzo. He's right. You can't."

"I'm going to get my father's letter, even if I have to go alone. Besides, we have to go back. General Washington's letter to Colonel De Gálvez was in my saddlebags. We need to get it before my grandfather hands it over to the British."

If he hasn't already, I silently added.

A collective groan went up.

Gibson looked at William with resignation. "I didn't have anything better to do tonight. What about you?"

Chapter Twenty-Nine

Gibson, William Linn, Calderón, and I left our horses tied to a tree at the edge of the plantation and stole toward the mansion. We tested several windows until we found one unlatched. For the second time in twenty-four hours, I entered my grandfather's house, but this time, like a thief in the night.

No one said a word as we padded down the hallway with our pistols drawn and primed. We eased open door after door until we found my grandfather asleep on a canopy bed.

It surprised me that no servants slept in the "big house" to wait on him should he need something in the middle of the night.

Gibson put a pistol to my grandfather's head while I clamped my hand over his mouth and Calderón pinned his arms.

"Don't move," I warned. By this time William had lit a candle. "I came back for my possessions," I told my grandfather.

Eyes filled with terror peered up at me.

"Don't make a sound." I eased my hand from his mouth. "Get up."

He did.

"First," I said, "I want my father's medical bag and other things."

His mouth twitched with disgust. "They're in the pantry downstairs. Take them and go. I don't care a fig about them." He acted brave, but there was fear in his eyes.

Gibson sent Calderón to fetch them.

Calderón lit a second candle, cupped his hand around the flame to protect it from a draft, and left.

We led my grandfather downstairs to the study and the safe containing my father's letter.

"Open the safe," I ordered.

"No."

"Open it," I snarled. "All I want is the letter."

"I destroyed it."

"You lie. I saw you put it in the safe." I pointed toward King George's portrait. "Open it." I gave him a spiteful push forward.

"No."

"Let him be, Lorenzo," Gibson said. He rubbed his fingers together, put his ear to the safe, and spun the dial, listening carefully for the tumblers to fall into place. "Not much of a safe, Your Honor. Hope you don't keep important documents in here." He opened the door.

"By all that's holy," Calderón softly exclaimed in dismay. He had returned from the pantry with my possessions in time to witness Gibson's safe-breaking talents in action.

Gibson grinned. "The fruits of a misspent youth."

"This is all I found," Calderón said, indicating my father's medical bag and my rawhide pouch.

Where were my saddlebags and Washington's letter?

I reached inside the safe. A grin stretched across my face when I pulled out Papá's letter.

"Take the damn thing!" my grandfather said, his tone defiant. "If you take me to court, you will only embarrass yourself. Why do you think I didn't destroy it? Because I knew I could use it against you if need be."

"What are you talking about?" I demanded.

"I received your father's letter saying he was coming home. I looked forward to seeing him beg me to reinstate him in the will. And I would have. All he had to do was disavow that woman and you."

"*That woman*," I said sarcastically, "was my mother."

"That woman," my grandfather said, echoing my tone, "was a trollop who bewitched Jack."

I took a menacing step toward my grandfather, but Gibson stepped in the way.

"This is getting us nowhere," Gibson said in a calm voice.

I had to know what the letter contained, so I opened it on the spot and tilted it toward the candlelight.

Father, a letter from me after all these years must surprise you. I wouldn't have written you now, except that I find myself with no way out. I am dying of consumption. By the time you read this, I shall be dead. My dying wish is that you make Lorenzo your legal heir.

I have trained my son to be a physician. He wishes to become a soldier. I have always believed a man should follow his heart wherever it leads him. That's why I took Mariana and Lorenzo to Mexico.

Father, I beg that you grant a dying man his final wish. The time has come to put our differences behind us. I ask that you accept Lorenzo as your flesh and blood. His mother and I were legally married in New Spain. I further ask that you give him his rightful inheritance.

Jack

"I will never acknowledge a half-breed bastard as my grandson," my grandfather snarled.

I stared at the words "legally married in New Spain." They leaped off the page. I read and reread them. I was born in Virginia before my parents moved to New Spain. That meant I was born before they had married.

The signature was the only part of the letter in my father's handwriting. Papá had dictated the letter to a monk in San Antonio one night while I slept. Now I knew why.

And I recalled what Papá said just before he died: "I was right to take you and your mother from Virginia."

He had taken us to a land where my mother and I would blend in, where no one would know he and my mother had married after I was born, where I wouldn't have to live with the stigma of illegitimacy.

I felt like all the blood had rushed out of me. The room began to spin. And then I recalled my grandfather's note: "Come home, Jack, and we will work out the differences between us." It wasn't a note suggesting forgiveness. My father had misinterpreted the message. In a sudden flash, I now knew that my grandfather wished for Papá to return so he could grovel. My grandfather's note hadn't mentioned me at all. No wonder he sold me to a press gang. I was an embarrassment and a threat to his property.

"So now you know the truth about your parents," my grandfather growled.

Somehow I managed to say, "That doesn't change the fact that I am your grandson and always will be."

"You are an accident of birth. Your mother had no business mixing her blood with ours. I rue the day Jack met her."

Nothing else he said registered. On unsteady legs, I headed toward the door and found my way outside.

A cold wind slapped me in the face when I reached the back porch. It brought me back to the present. After a moment, I realized someone had joined me. I glanced to my left.

Calderón bit his lower lip; his gaze focused on the starry sky. "I know exactly how you feel, Lorenzo. It stings at first, but you'll get over it. You're the same man you were yesterday. You just know something about yourself and your parents you didn't know before."

"You don't understand," I muttered, shaking my head.

"I understand too well. Remember asking me if I was related to King Carlos?" Calderón smiled bitterly. "He's my father."

Shock ran through me. When I twisted toward him, I found Calderón's jaw clenched, his head bowed.

"My mother was the king's mistress. I served as page in the Royal Palace until the queen noticed the indecent resemblance between me and her husband. There was an attempt on my life. That's why the king sent me to New Orleans."

A noise behind us drew our attention.

Gibson and Linn ran toward us carrying my possessions. "Gentlemen," Gibson said, "I suggest we get out of here on the double. William and I tied Judge Bannister up and left him gagged in the library. One of his slaves will find him tomorrow and release him. He'll probably fabricate a story about a robbery."

I knew what Gibson was thinking. My grandfather had worked hard to keep me a secret. He would never say that his illegitimate half-breed grandson had come back for a showdown. Pistols at the ready, we dashed away toward the edge of the plantation. Just as we passed the stable, a figure holding a lantern stepped out of the dark.

Chapter Thirty

On instinct we raised our pistols and thumbed back the hammers.

"Lord have mercy! Don't shoot. It's just me. Cincinnatus." He looked straight at me. "I gotta talk to you."

We lowered our weapons.

Glancing about nervously, he motioned us into a multi-stalled stable. Horses, disturbed by our presence, snorted at us and shifted nervously.

"William," Gibson whispered, "keep a lookout at that door." He pointed to the far end of the stable. "Calderón, go to the other exit."

William Linn and Calderón dutifully obeyed.

Cincinnatus led us into an empty stall and hung the lantern on a peg. "You're Jack's son, aren't you?" he said to me in muted tones.

"Yes." I offered my hand, which he took. "I'm glad to meet you finally. Papá talked about you often."

My remark brought a smile to his face. "I knew you was his boy. You don't look much like him, 'cept for the straight hair, but you walk like him, talk like him. You got your mama's face." The elderly black man glanced over his shoulder. "Ain't safe for you here. We gotta get you outta Virginia. The sooner, the better."

"The man's right," Gibson whispered.

"I was afraid Judge Bannister had killed you," Cincinnatus went on. "I saw you go in the big house. Next thing I know, he comes to the stable and tells me to get his carriage ready. Then he drives off with your horse tied to the back of the carriage. He comes back a little later, but your horse is gone. He was up to something. Yes, siree. That's why I hid your things soon as I unsaddled your horse."

I straightened. "You have my letters?"

The air crackled with excitement. Now I knew who had General Washington's letter as well.

He led us to a large wooden tack box. "Put everything in here." Stooping over, he opened the lid and pushed aside brushes, curry combs, and horse accessories of all kinds. At the very bottom rested my saddlebags and raccoonskin haversack with Papá's correspondence and Eugenie's love letters.

I unbuckled the saddlebags, took out *Gerald's Herbal*, opened it, and breathed a long sigh of relief to see General Washington's letter. "Thank you." I looked deep into his watery, black eyes. "Did you know Papá's gone?"

"I figured so when I saw you arrive alone. When did he pass away?"

"Last August."

Cincinnatus pinched the bridge of his nose and lowered his head. "Jack was like my own boy. He taught me how to read. Did he tell you that?"

"Yes."

"He was about eight years old at the time. Wasn't supposed to, but he did anyway. It was our secret. And that was the summer he promised, 'I'll see you free, Cincinnatus. One way or the other.'"

A light went on inside my head. "So that explains it. The day before Papá passed away, he was delirious and mumbled something about not keeping his promise to you." I choked back a sob. Now Papá could never make good on the promise. But I could. I thought about the money in my saddlebags. "I'll buy your freedom."

Cincinnatus offered me a bitter smile. "The judge won't sell. Your daddy tried that, but Judge Bannister wouldn't allow it. Jack did what he could. I don't fault him none. I'm just glad he got away from here." His face grew even sadder. "I was there the day he argued with Judge Bannister. What his father did was wrong. Dead wrong."

I gave him a sympathetic nod. "Papá never talked much about that. It always choked him up."

"It was a terrible fight," Cincinnatus said. "Whole plantation heard it. Judge Bannister and Jack argued about you and your mama. The judge said he would sell you and your mama unless Jack joined the king's navy. Jack was going to do it, too, but I talked him out of it. I knew you couldn't trust the judge as far as you could throw him. Jack and me decided there was only one thing to do—escape to New Spain where you and your mama could live free."

I stared at Cincinnatus. "What do you mean?"

"Oh, my God," Gibson said in slow understanding. He turned his wide-eyed gaze toward me. "Oh, my God," he repeated. "Lorenzo . . . Your mother was a slave."

Head spinning, knees wobbling, I could only stare at him in confusion.

"Jack met your mother the day a Mexican gentleman visited the plantation on business," Cincinnatus said. "He brought his daughter, Mariana. He had fathered her off one of his slaves."

Rubbing the nape of his neck, Gibson muttered an oath in French. He tilted his head back and frowned in concentration. "If Lorenzo's mother was a mulatto, that would make him a quadroon."

"Quadroon?" I asked. "What's that?"

"Someone who is a quarter black," Gibson answered. "Legally, you're a slave."

"What?" I cried, still not understanding. "I'm no man's slave."

"You belong to your grandfather," Cincinnatus said. "The Mexican had money trouble. He sold Mariana to Judge Bannister."

"But my father was free," I protested.

"Lorenzo," Gibson said, placing his hand on my shoulder, "if your mother was a slave, it makes no difference if your father was free or not. By coming upriver, you've put yourself in slavery. If I had known this, I'd never have allowed you to endanger yourself. I'm sorry. I never once suspected."

Cincinnatus straightened. "If you never suspected . . ." He pivoted toward me. "You been passing for white. You're light enough. You keep on doing it."

I looked at Cincinnatus aghast. My mind was still reeling. "What? No!"

"You listen to me," Cincinnatus snapped. "Do it! Ain't nothing wrong with being black. I ain't saying that. I don't want to be white, but I sure wish I had the *privileges* of being white."

"Lorenzo, you wouldn't be doing anything you haven't already done," Gibson gently pointed out. "For years. Your father raised you in a land where you and your mother would blend in. He trained you to be a physician. He never intended to tell you what he had done or why he did it. Even on his death bed, when he knew time was short, he remained silent to protect you."

"But why did he send me to Virginia and put me into slavery?"

"I don't know," Gibson said.

The answer leaped to mind. "Because my grandfather wrote him and suggested they put the past behind them. My father thought my grandfather had forgiven him at last."

Nodding slowly, Gibson said, "The ugly truth is this. When he took you and your mother, he stole your grandfather's property. Your grandfather had the law on his side, and he knew it."

I started to protest, but Gibson's uplifted hand stopped me.

"Slavery is immoral and I don't condone it, but it is legal. No doubt, your father thought your grandfather was ready to accept you as his legal heir. If Judge Bannister designated you as such in his will, then you would inherit the plantation."

"And then Jack could keep his promise," Cincinnatus added. "He said he was going to free us after the judge died." He paused. "But the old goat outlived Jack. For years, we've kept the promise alive here." At this point, Cincinnatus's eyes grew moist. He touched his chest, right over his heart. "Now, you're our only hope. We're counting on you."

An entire plantation depended on me to free them. Oh, God! How was I to do that? My brain was a confusion of ideas jumbling around, slamming into each other, none of them making sense. "How many slaves will two hundred dollars buy?"

Gibson frowned at me. "Probably one." His face lit with understanding. "Lorenzo," he said, laying a gentle hand on my shoulder, "your grandfather has made it clear that he will never accept you. He will never see you as anything but a slave. He certainly will never sell Cincinnatus to you. Your grandfather can hire bounty hunters to find you and bring you back. You must go to New Orleans right away and buy your freedom papers."

I let out a long groan. Gibson was right. My grandfather had already sold me once to a British press gang. He would sell me again. Anything to be rid of me.

"Look, Gator. Honor is its own reward. Sometimes, we must do things to satisfy political law, and in this case, an immoral law. In Virginia, you are under English law. You can do nothing to force your grandfather to sell you freedom papers. But in New Orleans, you are under Spanish law. There, you can take Judge Bannister to court and force a sale."

Suddenly, all I could think of was returning to New Orleans. But then, something occurred to me. "If that's so, then Papá must have forced my grandfather to sell me and my mother our freedom when we reached New Spain."

Gibson looked me straight in the eye. "No. Think about it a moment. Did you find freedom papers in the things your father left behind?"

I shook my head. I had gone through all his papers.

"To force a sale, your father had to go to court. He was on the run. If he'd been discovered, he would have gone to jail, and you and your mother would have been sent back to the plantation. Under the circumstances, going to court would have been the last thing he would have done."

I blew out a long sigh and leaned my head against a post. Suddenly I recalled something Calderón had said on the flatboats. When I told him Papá and I had traveled around a lot, he remarked, "Sounds like you two were running from the law."

Papá was. Only I didn't know it.

I looked at Gibson. "I am my grandfather's only rightful heir. I can take him to court. Not here, but in New Spain. If I inherit his property and his slaves, I can free them all." That, I thought with a silent, ironic laugh, was one of the privileges of being white. "I've got to get back to New Orleans."

"That's right," Gibson said. "We've stayed here too long as is."

"Goodbye," I said to Cincinnatus. "I'll do what I can to free us."

Cincinnatus gave my hand a long shake. "I knew you was Jack's boy."

"Uh, by the way," Gibson said, "we left the judge tied up in the study."

Cincinnatus's eyes glowed with delight. "'Spect I'll be awful busy tomorrow. Don't suppose I'll have any reason to go into the big house until, oh, ten . . . no, eleven o'clock."

We grinned at each other. Gibson and I shook his hand and left.

Gibson whistled to Calderón and William Linn, signaling them to rejoin us.

With the stomping and snorting of horses, I wondered how much they had heard of our conversation. I searched their faces. They looked at me the same way as before. Either they hadn't heard Cincinnatus's revelations, or it didn't matter.

Chapter Thirty-One

On the way back to camp, I had plenty of time to think. Calderón and William Linn rode ahead, Gibson and I rode behind.

I suddenly realized this whole thing—the slavery issue, the war against King George—was personal now. So what was my role to be?

A plan came to mind, and the more it ballooned, the better I liked it. Back in New Orleans, I could buy slaves from my grandfather's plantation. I would have to start small, free as many as my finances would allow. Cincinnatus was right. My grandfather would never sell to me. Still, I would find a way. And with Eugenie's help and support . . .

I reined in my horse. What would Eugenie think about all this?

Major Gibson, who rode beside me, stopped.

I swallowed hard and asked, "What about Eugenie?"

"What about her?"

"What do I tell her?"

"I've found the truth usually works best."

Calderón and William Linn, deep in conversation, continued on for a few yards before they stopped and twisted around in their saddles. They looked at each other, shrugged, and continued on.

"Look, Lorenzo," Gibson, said when Calderón and William Linn were out of earshot, "Eugenie's French. The French are open-minded. When my brother John married an Indian woman, everyone worried about my grandmother's reaction. She's French nobility, you see. One day, I visited Grandmama in Philadelphia. She cornered me and asked me straight out why everyone was so secretive about John's wife. Why didn't John's wife come to visit? I told her the truth. Grandmama breathed a sigh of relief. '*Mon Dieu!*' she exclaimed. 'She's Indian. Is that all? The way everyone was acting, I thought she was British.'"

I laughed at Gibson's anecdote, then sobered. "Are you saying it won't matter to Eugenie?"

"Like I said, she's French. I bet you a Spanish pillar dollar it won't."

I didn't take the bet and I prayed he was right.

"If you plan to marry Eugenie, tell her the whole story. Keeping secrets is no way to start a marriage."

By the time we spotted the Lambs' campfire and rejoined Calderón and William Linn, my head had cleared, but it wasn't until I saw Red that the solution to my dilemma burst into my brain. I knew exactly what to do.

"Red, old buddy," I said, lapping my arm around his shoulder. "Would you do me a big favor?"

He eyed me suspiciously and gave a cautious answer. "Depends on the favor."

"If I gave you two hundred dollars, would you buy me a slave?"

Red's nostrils flared. He shook off my arm and let out a long string of expletives. "No, I wouldn't. Slavery ain't right, and I won't have any part of it."

"No, no," I said, waving my hands frantically. "You misunderstand me. I want you to buy a man and send him to New Orleans so I can give him his freedom."

For a long moment, no one moved. Tension hung in the air. Gibson swiveled toward me, as did Linn and Calderón.

"Do it, Red." Gibson regarded me through narrowed eyes.

I stared straight back at him. "Sometimes there are

things greater than ourselves at stake. My father knew that, and that's why he sent me to Virginia. He had a plan and I'll see it done."

Gibson blinked at me. "By God, I believe you will."

I turned to Red. "The slave I want you to buy belongs to my grandfather. His name is Cincinnatus."

Over a supper of beans and potatoes, Red and I put our heads together and planned out what we would do. Whenever I could, I would send him a bank draft. He would buy a slave under his name, put that person on a ship bound for New Orleans, and I would be waiting on the pier with freedom papers in hand.

"Lorenzo," Gibson said, "do you know how difficult it will be to save two hundred dollars?"

"Or how many years it will take to free them all?" Calderón asked.

William Linn shook his head. "An admirable plan, Lorenzo. I fear slavery will tear this country apart some day. Some delegates wanted to put an anti-slavery clause in the Declaration of Independence, but others refused to agree to that, so it was taken out."

I stared at him in disbelief. "How can we fight for freedom but keep people in slavery?"

No one had an answer to that.

Chapter Thirty-Two

Calderón and I returned to New Orleans on a night in late June. We stood in front of Colonel De Gálvez's house, staring at each other. Light from a full moon reflected off the darkened windowpanes. The house showed no hint of life.

"He could be at the barracks," Calderón suggested.

In unison, we grinned at each other and said, "He's at the widow's house."

We dashed away. Five minutes later, we stood in her foyer, announcing ourselves to the butler. I had hardly spoken my name when someone let out a squeal.

"Lorenzo!" Eugenie rushed toward me and leaped into my open arms.

We kissed.

Calderón cleared his throat. "Uh, Lorenzo . . ."

I ignored him and kept on kissing Eugenie.

He cleared his throat again and tapped me on the shoulder.

When Eugenie and I finally separated, I saw Colonel De Gálvez before me, arm in arm with the widow. He pulled me to him in a Spanish embrace, then did the same to Calderón.

The most amazing thing had happened since I'd been gone. Either the colonel had shrunk two inches or I had grown. We were now eye to eye.

Everyone laughed, hugged, asked questions at the same time until, finally, the widow raised her voice over the din.

"You two look hungry. Join us in the dining room."

Calderón and I were ravenous. Our timing couldn't have been better. The mouth-watering aroma of seafood drifted from the dining room. A supper of broiled shrimp and oysters and clams, the food I had missed so much. What a delicious welcome.

"Tell me about your visit with your grandfather," Eugenie remarked as she looped her arm around my elbow.

I stopped dead and looked deep into her wide, green eyes. A sudden heaviness pressed on my chest.

"Lorenzo, what's the matter? What happened in Virginia?"

Colonel De Gálvez and the widow paused in the doorway and smiled back at us.

The temperature in the room seemed to climb higher and higher. Surrounded by the people I loved most in the world, I still found myself unable to say the words. I looked to Calderón for help.

"Tell her, Lorenzo. In the meantime, I'll explain everything to the colonel."

I knew he was right. It had been hard enough telling Calderón all I had learned from Cincinnatus. Could I get the words out now and could I say them right?

"Eugenie . . ." I began.

"Not here, you dolt," Calderón gently scolded, putting his hands on my back and shoving me toward the courtyard. He glanced at me over his shoulder and hurried back to the dining room.

Once outside, Eugenie and I sat side by side on a wooden bench. How I had missed her. But now that I was with her, smelling her scent, close to her warmth, I feared her reaction to my news.

She took my hand and caressed it.

Overhead, starlight lit the welcome sight of Spanish moss hanging from a cypress tree. It reminded me of Red's uncombed beard.

I avoided her eyes. Focusing on a magnolia, I stammered out the story. I concluded by saying, "That's the whole story. At first, I thought I'd buy my freedom with the money I made as a medic, but I gave it to Red so he could free Cincinnatus. He should be arriving here any time." I took a deep breath.

She absorbed it all in silence, never once interrupting to ask a question, then her expression grew troubled. "Will your grandfather have any legal claim to our children?"

My heart was beating wildly. "Our children," she had said. "No. If the mother is free, the children are automatically free. Does this mean it doesn't matter to you?" I asked, hope coursing through me.

She tilted her head prettily. "Well, of course, it doesn't. I never imagined I would marry someone British." She gave an exaggerated shudder. "I despise the British."

I couldn't help but laugh. "I plan to join the army and fight for American freedom. Does that erase the sin of having British blood in my veins?"

"It's a start."

"Will you marry me when the war is over?"

"No."

Surprised, I pulled back.

She leaned closer. "I don't want to wait that long."

Whether I kissed her or she kissed me is debatable. I don't remember much after that. Except that we stayed so long in the courtyard, Colonel De Gálvez, the widow, and Calderón had to come get us.

"Well?" Calderón demanded, barely able to contain himself. "We're waiting. Food's getting cold."

"Eugenie and I are getting married."

We received their congratulations, then headed to the dining room.

Before we took our seats, Colonel De Gálvez leaned toward me and said under his breath, "Lieutenant Calderón explained the problem. I'll start the legal paperwork to secure your freedom papers . . ."

"Sir, I'd prefer that you didn't."

"Why not?" he asked.

"If I am found with freedom papers on me, society will treat me differently. Right now, I have all the privileges of being white. I intend to use them to free others." I told the colonel about Cincinnatus's advice to "pass for white."

Colonel De Gálvez shook his head. "But if someone learns the truth and you have no freedom papers . . ."

"That's a danger I'll have to live with."

"No, Lorenzo. You must have documented proof you are a free man. I shall procure them for you and lock them in my safe." He paused. "And I shall pray I need never remove them." He shook his head. "What a world we live in!"

"Maybe we can leave it a little better for our children."

The colonel and I sat at the table under a blazing chandelier.

"Brace yourself. It's seafood again," Colonel De Gálvez whispered. "What I wouldn't give for a big, juicy Texas steak. I haven't had one in years."

"Bernardo!" the widow scolded. "I heard that."

"I'm sorry, dear, I . . . I . . ."

I jumped in to rescue him. "I know exactly what he means. On the trip up the Mississippi, it seemed like trout and perch were all we ate." I rubbed my hand over my chin. "You know, if I made it all the way from San Antonio in a whole skin, a herd of longhorns could, too."

For a long moment, Colonel De Gálvez stared at me. "By all that's holy, they could."

"I'm glad you said that. General Washington wants to buy food for the Continental Army." I gave him Washington's letter.

"So does the Continental Congress," the colonel said. "I received a letter from Patrick Henry last week on the same subject."

"Someone could drive cattle east from San Antonio," I suggested, warming to the subject, "and ship them north from here."

Eugenie placed her hand on my arm. "What a marvelous idea."

"Have you ever been on a cattle drive?" Colonel De Gálvez asked with deep interest.

"In San Antonio, I helped a friend with his livestock from time to time."

"Lorenzo!" the widow exclaimed. "You were a *vaquero*! How exciting!"

Colonel De Gálvez's lips curled in a diabolical smile. I knew that smile. It meant trouble. "The more I think about Lorenzo's idea, the better I like it. Lieutenant Calderón, how soon could your company be ready to head out?"

Calderón froze with a forkful of shrimp halfway to his mouth. His eyes darted toward me and shot me a "you-and-your-big-mouth" look. "I . . . I'd need to find out if any of my men are *vaqueros*," he stammered out. "If it please Your Excellency, Lorenzo should go along as a scout. He knows the trail firsthand, and by the time everything's ready, he'll be sixteen and ready to use this." He unbuttoned his jacket, reached inside, and pulled out two pieces of parchment neatly folded in thirds.

All heads swiveled toward him, mine included.

"Lorenzo," he began, "when we were in General Washington's camp, he gave me a letter and asked me to give it to you when you turned sixteen. A little early." He shrugged. "Happy returns of the day," he said, passing it to me. "The second letter is from Major Gibson."

Frowning at Calderón, I opened General Washington's letter and scanned only the first few lines before I leaped up, making my chair clatter to the floor.

A captaincy in the Continental Army. With Major Gibson as my commanding officer. I was to be the liaison between General Washington and Colonel De Gálvez.

"Yahoo!" I exclaimed. "It's official now. I'm one of Gibson's Lambs."

Calderón assumed a mock serious look. "An officer must maintain some semblance of decorum."

Eugenie leaned toward me and whispered in my ear, "Captain Lorenzo Bannister. I like the sound of that."

So did I. I tore into Major Gibson's letter.

It welcomed me to his command. Due to his recent promotion to major, he was now a staff officer and was turning the Lambs over to me and William Linn. Patrick Henry would soon send William and a squad of Lambs to Boonesborough to assist the harrassed Kentuckians there. The remainder would come downriver to New Orleans by flatboat.

"My God!" I muttered in disbelief. "I'm in charge of Gibson's Lambs."

"Now they're your Lambs," Calderón pointed out.

In July, I turned sixteen. With a steady job and a bright future in the military, I could marry Eugenie, raise a family, and fight for freedom for all Americans.

I barely heard the discussion from that point on. Overcome with joy, I leaned back and took a sip of tea. Tea. Papá's favorite drink. I smiled at the memory. It still hurt to think about Papá. Would the pain and sorrow of losing him ever lessen?

I was now Captain Lorenzo Bannister of the Continental Army, a special envoy for General Washington. As I said the words to myself, I imagined Papá's joy in heaven as he looked down and watched me serve the cause of liberty.